Best Wishes

Susan Shea

Willies Passions

Willies Passions

Susan These

To order additional copies of this book, contact:
Xlibris Corporation
1-888-795-4274
www.Xlibris.com
Orders@Xlibris.com
109846

TABLE OF CONTENTS

SECTION II – NEW YEARS IN THE WILDERNESS

SECTION III – THE KOOTENAYS

N.B. All the art reproduced in this book is by Wilma

Five Generations
L to R: Heidi (eldest granddaughter), Willie (photograph), Granny Noreen
holding great-great grandson Seth, and Susie

Dedication

*This book is dedicated
to the memory of Wilma
my Mother and Best Friend*

AUTHOR'S NOTE

A year after my Mothers' death I received a box in which her personal journals and notes of her adventures through the years had been put. I spent a great deal of time reading with both tears and laughter.

I have been blessed to have communicated with my Mothers spirit and true to form she has not lost her sense of humor. As she so jokingly put it we have done many things together in the land of the living why not now. "I am the ghost and you are the writer, if you enjoyed reading this as much as you say then lets do it!"

With this comment what is a daughter to do? Write a short story of my Mothers life? Impossible. Nothing is impossible just watch.

Wilma is an autobiography—its characters are actual individuals taken from my mother's notes. Her life was an inspiration to all who knew her. The book follows her life at approximately twenty year intervals. The stories are her, I am just the one to have the honor of sharing it with those who appreciate nature and the beauties of British Columbia.

I hope you enjoy reading this book on some of Wilmas' life as much as I enjoyed writing it.

- Susie -

WILMA ELLEN JOYCE

WIFE, MOTHER, GRANDMOTHER, DAUGHTER, SISTER, AUNT AND FRIEND!

---

*W*hat can you say about Wilma?

Anyone that knew her will remember her smiling face, tender touches loving hugs and laughter.

Loving life as she lived life—to the fullest.

Always there to listen to your problems, happy times and sad times, in confidence and offer advice if asked for it.

The first to a dance and the last to leave, Wilma was the party.

She loved her smokes and she loved her drink. There were times she would be giving Russ the itinerary for the dances while trying to lead John around the dance floor. The only person she could ever dance beautifully with was Norm. They truly had a wonderful but all too short life together.

Wilma was born in Campbell River March 14, 1936 (Thankyou Granny for the precious gift you gave to us).

At the young age of 17 she married Thomas McLeod known to everyone as "TUCK". As a devoted wife and dedicated mother she raised 4 children.

Susie, Tommy, Marina and Mark. As a special Mother she always saw to it that there was a birthday party for each no matter where we were.

At Christmas time we would all sit huddled close while she read us her legacy of "Annie & Willies Prayer". Never a night would go by that she would not come in to our rooms with a hug and a kiss goodnight.

She taught us the true values of life, the gift of love and gave us the faith of hope.

During the 33 years of marriage to Tuck her occupation was wife and fulltime mother. Her special interests were painting, hiking, trail biking, cooking, tracing our family tree and reading.

After Tucks sudden death she was a lost soul. Although she had the love of her family and friends she was lost.

Wilma and Susie took a brief trip to Europe and after traveling with dear friends and visiting old friends she returned home with a renewed outlook on life.

Shortly after her return she met up with her first love—she was 6 years old when she first fell in love with Norm. Thank heaven above for life long friends.

Wilma and Norman were married a year and a half after her sad period in life. They celebrated their marriage in the presence of family and friends of a lifetime. This truly was one of the happiest times of her life. Her soul was renewed once again.

Together Willie and Norm were inseparable. It was hard to keep up with these two between their days of traveling around every little backroad of this province she so dearly loved. The days of mushroom picking, boating and fishing up the inlet, with a little starter fluid for both the boat and Wilma, were always full of laughs and jokes.

While boating up the inlet she would on occasion bring out her accordion and serenade the fish. It must have worked because there was always fresh cod and snapper to eat. Wilma and Norm also had the art of shrimping down to an art. They were quite a team to watch. Always a pleasure.

We will miss the days of family dinners and listening to Willie and John argue over who was going to make the gravy or who was cheating at dirty board.

Eight wonderful years with Norm was the gift of life he gave to her. She was not ready to go to the next life but we know that she is waiting for us.

It was five weeks when Wilma was diagnosed with cancer of the lung which had spread to the brain until her death. With shock she phoned all her loved ones to tell them the news, with lots of tears she started the fight of her life.

Even in treatment of chemotherapy and radiation she could smile and joke, telling the nurses she should have had her brain zapped years ago!

Wilma decided that she had to make a trip to see friends of ours in their time of sorrow as well as make a trip to Alberta to see where Marina was living (she knew this was important to Marina). Tom, flying across Canada to visit with Mom, is now the chauffeur to the most special lady of our lives.

Unfortunately she only made the trip halfway. Upon her return to Lions Gate Hospital she spent 5 courageous days of fighting to stay with us. It has been said that when one passes away, if they have one true friend by their side they have done extremely well in life. Wilma had six loved ones by her side which is an indication of her success in life.

We'll all be together again one day and we know she would not want us to be sad, she would want us to carry on because life is precious.

Wilma would be overwhelmed to think that so many people cared and loved her as we did.

L to R: Mark, Marina, Tom, Susie

SECTION I

WEST COAST WATERS

Chapter 1

THE HOMECOMING

---

*T*he Norseman, a small three-passenger plane, flew high above great masses of swirling fog, headed toward its remote destination, Queen's Cove, on the wild west coast of Vancouver Island. As it neared the Cove all fog vanished, revealing a tiny fishing settlement in the wilderness. Making silvery streaks in the bright afternoon sunshine, the plane soon settled on the shimmering water. A large dumpy rowboat pulled alongside.

"Hello there, Jim" I heard my father's voice call. "Got my daughter aboard this trip?"

"Sure have Moody! Here she is."

Then I was carefully lifted over the plane's side into the boat, where I was tearfully greeted by my father, whom I had not seen for six years. I had been living with my mother on Cortez Island. I was fourteen years old, and felt lost.

Soon we clambered aboard the large fish camp which was to become my home. There I was met by my stepmother Olive, a small dark woman, and her two small children, my half-brother and half-sister. The camp was a large floating two-storey building, with our home and the store in the top storey and accommodation for buying fish in the bottom.

The hundreds of fish boats, which sold their fish to the camp in the spring and summer months, had now dwindled to a mere few. The fish packer, which made regular twice a week stops in spring and summer, now visited us only once a week to bring us mail, groceries and supplies for the small store which each camp operated.

This life I soon found was going to be very hard to adjust to, with no friends my own age. I still felt lost and rather lonely. Most of the day I was kept busy helping with the housework and children, but time still hung on my hands. I soon got to know everyone in the settlement. They were friendly people who made me feel very welcome, but I longed for the friends I had always known, and the road where I had played as a child.

When September came, I felt that I should be with my friends at school, but there I sat alone in a bedroom with great mounds of grade ten correspondence lessons for me. Instead of getting to work, I often sat in a dream-like trance, picturing myself back among my friends. How lucky they were, I thought, to be able to go to school.

Evenings spent in this kind of study were not unhappy, just tedious and unreal. The happy evenings were those when Dad had time to tell me stories of incidents that had happened in this lonely cove—such as the story of the smart rat. Trying to outsmart this rat had kept dad busy most of one winter.

Chapter 2

OUR SEA MONSTER

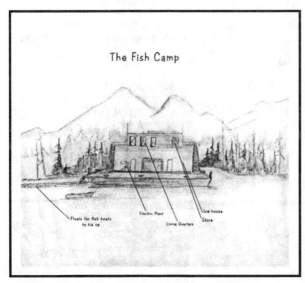

The Fish Camp

Floats for fish boats to tie up · Electric Plant · Living Quarters · Ice house · Store

*E*ach camp has an "ice house" to keep the fish frozen or at least cold until the packer boat picks them up. In the winter, with no fish, the ice house is swept clean, except for a small mound of crushed ice to keep milk and meat cold.

One winter a rat swam from shore and decided to take up residence in father's ice house and make a nest there.

She could easily pull the tabs from the milk bottles and drink the cream down as far as her tongue would reach. Father tried putting poison in one or two bottles, hoping this would finish off the unwelcome guest, but this didn't work. The rat would lift the tabs from the poisoned bottles, but not a drop of the milk would she drink.

Father tried dozens of different traps that various people recommended. The ordinary rat trap was much too simple. The rat would pull a piece of rope or wood over the trap until it sprung, then she would eat the bait! Father walked the floors at night, trying to think of a way to outsmart this little rodent, but he could not find one. Finally he decided that the only thing he could do was to starve her to death, by keeping all food out of the ice house for some weeks. In the spring he found the remains of the nest, built of odds and ends, at the end of a tunnel through the crushed ice—but it had been abandoned long before . . . that smart rat just moved on!

Around the point from Queens Cove there was a small village of Indians who dealt at our camp store and at the other two as well. One family I remember well lived in a one-room shack on the edge of the beach. They had several children, and Mrs. Jay was expecting another. She had her baby by herself with three small children milling about, even though there was a large community with a doctor thirty miles away. Not long after the baby was born, Mr. Jay came to our store to buy some talcum powder for the baby. We didn't have the particular brand he had in mind so Mr. Jay went in his fish boat the thirty miles, to buy the kind of powder he wanted.

Most of the Indians were kind and thoughtful neighbors. At Christmas my stepmother made up parcels for the Indian children consisting of candy and gum which were greatly appreciated. The Chiefs' wife gave Olive and me the most beautiful presents, various sized bottles covered with tiny colorful beads, cleverly sewn in patterns representing different legends.

Christmas week was one big celebration. The packer brought parcels from far away relatives and friends, turkeys, liquor, and our own orders from the catalogs. Dad and I went out to get our

Christmas tree, and from among hundreds chose a large fir for the honor. Christmas Eve we decorated the tree with tinsel, lights and bright ornaments. Christmas morning my little half-siblings (Marion and Michael) got us all up early. Presents were opened and then vegetables peeled and the turkey made ready to pop into the oven.

We then dressed in our best finery, stepped into the rowboat—Dad taking good care of the wine bottle tucked under his arm—and set off to make the rounds of our neighbors to wish them all a very Merry Christmas.

New Years Eve one of our neighbors gave a party. I went along and stayed for a few hours, then rowed home so that dad and Olive could stay while I minded the children.

At the climax of the party the guests fired shotguns, rifles and automatics to welcome in the glad New Year, while I sat sadly at home, thinking of my friends in my old home town, as I imagined them dancing in their first long dresses.

I have told this story to many people, but I don't think any of them really believe me. I can hardly blame them. It was a cold, clear March day, there was still ice at the head of the cove. I

Looking down on the monster

was just getting dressed to row Olive across to another camp for afternoon tea.

Father was standing gazing idly out the window. All of a sudden he called, "What the hell's that?" We all ran to the window, practically pushing father to the. floor. The living quarters and store were upstairs, so we were looking down about twenty feet into the water at what appeared to be a creosote piling sticking out of the water, covered with barnacles. We had nearly decided that that's what it was, when we suddenly realized it was some sort of living animal.

Poking his head above the surface

Sea Monster

Father grabbed his gun and ran downstairs to get a closer look. As he did so the "piling" opened a great mouth at least eighteen inches in length to show off a great mass of pink tonsils.

The water was a pale delicate green and very clear, as the creature sank beneath the water again we got a perfect view of his body. Its neck seemed to be about eight feet long. It has an enormous wing-like fin protruding from each side of its body; then the piling-like body ended in a tail shaped like a salmons' approximately four feet wide.

Our monster was a good forty feet long, if not longer. He gradually moved along, very lazily, and stuck his awesome head through the ice at the end of the bay.

Olive and I finally gathered enough courage to get in the rowboat to go the tea party. When we told what we had seen there were giggles of laughter and our friends decided we had been frightened by a sea lion, so we let the subject drop.

I used to spend a great deal of time rowing my two small siblings around the bay, for something to do, and to keep them out of Dad and Olive's way. One bright afternoon as we climbed into the rowboat, I noticed only one small red troller tied to the floats, presumably a victim of engine trouble, because nearby there sat a very dejected young fisherman, grease from head to toe, quietly having a cigarette.

As we rowed by he said "Hello there—" and then something I could not hear. So I answered' "Mm-Hm—" which will pass in ordinary conversation, but sounds rather ridiculous shouted across the water. However, by that time we were too far past for him to say anything more, even if he hadn't felt snubbed. So I missed my first chance to meet my future husband. As a result we didn't meet until some months later.

Chapter 3

SEA OTTER COVE

---

*I*n the spring we were moved to an even more desolate place than Queens Cove. One morning the packer arrived to take us and the camp further up the West Coast. The crew worked hard getting all the cables undone from the shore, pulling up the anchors, and then getting good strong cables attached to the packer for the long tow.

We rode on the packer to our new home, Sea Otter Cove. We traveled all one day and night and arrived on a drizzly cold morning at a beautiful bay. On one side was a beach of pure white sand. At the head of the bay was a huge green field through which a trout stream emptied itself into the salt water. A strange sight in this uninhabited spot were many old houses fallen over and rotten, with tall alder trees growing through their roofs.

After much work our camp was very securely anchored into place, much more so than we had been at Queen's Cove, for the wind often blew at gale force in this exposed and lonely bay. Only the previous year after a wind storm with gusts up to 90 and 100 miles an hour, eight fish boats had been washed ashore and one of the fishermen drowned.

We were the Cove's only occupants until early summer, when another camp much smaller than ours was towed in, with one man left to operate it. Soon the fishermen arrived with their freshly painted boats, and there was ample work to keep all hands busy.

When we arrived we had no running water and had to keep rowing to shore to fetch water from a very small dam we had built.

Before long we had running water, hot and cold, our own electric lights, washing machine, iron and toaster, so we really were almost as comfortable as we had been at Queen's Cove.

We had our first experience of a wind storm before we had been there very long. One gray morning we found ourselves shouting at one another in order to make ourselves heard. We dared not open the doors as they would have been blown off their hinges. Our camp-hand, a boy of sixteen, slept downstairs. That morning he crawled on hands and knees to get upstairs, fearing that if he stood up the wind would make him lose his balance and topple him into the sea. It blew all day. Finally by evening the wind died down and all was well.

It didn't take us long to find there was an abundance of crabs up near the head of the cove. We straightened out large fish hooks and fastened them to long poles and speared the large moldy-looking creatures. Dropped them into boiling salty water for twenty minutes, they emerged pinky orange and were delicious.

We often went trout fishing, which meant a long hike up the bank of the creek to get the larger trout. There were many bear dens, and we had to be careful not to fall in them. The bear usually chose a large stump and would dig a great cave like hole beneath it for a long winters sleep and we had no wish to disturb him.

Wild animals in the Cove were plentiful. There were bears, cougars, mink, raccoons and many bald-headed eagles made their nests in the tall lifeless trees.

Just up behind where we had built our small dam when we first arrived, we found a cougars' homing place.

There were great stacks of bones, mainly deer, I think, and a lot of short brown pieces of fur. We found out later that a cougar plucks the hair or fur from his kill before he eats it.

One night Tim, Father's helper, and Tuck, a handsome young fisherman lately arrived at the Cove, rowed over to a tiny island near the mouth of the Cove and captured an enormous fat raccoon. Despite his girth he was a tricky fighter. After quite a struggle they got him cornered in a hollow log near the waters edge. One man stood at each end of the log with a heavy burlap sack. The tide was coming in, so Mr. Coon had to drown or take a chance on the unknown, the sack. He chose the sack, and was soon brought over to our camp and put in a large box with thin slate nailed across. He devoured all the freshly caught trout we had on board and any other fish we'd give him. Although greedy he was quite fastidious in his way, and thoroughly scrubbed every fish in water we had placed in an old tobacco can. You didn't dare put your hand too close, or he'd have gladly taken that along also. He ate well while he stayed with us. It wasn't for long, we soon let him go, for he was literally eating us out of fish. When we released him he swam very quickly back to his old home, apparently, in spite of all his greed—very glad to escape from all the curious inquiring eyes.

One Labour Day, when all the fishing fleet was tied up to the dock because the weather was too rough to fish, an Indian fisherman decided to take a walk through the woods, in the hope of getting a deer for a little fresh meat. With his trusty 22 in hand, he sauntered along a deer trail on the edge of a high bluff near the waters edge. He had not gone far when like a bolt of lightning a dark object sprang from the trees above and landed a few feet in front of him. It was a cougar. To the terrified man it looked as big as a horse.

It quickly turned and crouched on its stomach, ready to spring. The Indian came to his senses, and fired eight tiny bullets into the cougars' head, turned, and ran as fast as his short legs could carry him to his boat; and rowed as fast as possible, not just till he was out of danger, but all the way to the camp. The other fishermen said he was the whitest Indian they had ever seen.

The next day several men went with the Indian and brought the cougar back to camp. From the nose tip to tail tip he measured nine feet. They skinned the cougar and sent the ears away, so that the Indian would collect his forty dollars bounty.

After that incident we stuck to our crab fishing by the shore. We had bought crab pots, which are large baskets—like bells, made with a metal rim around the top and net sides and bottoms. We tied a piece of fish or a whole fish in the bottom. A long rope was then brought to the surface and a wooden buoy attached. When the crabs flocked into the pots to eat the bait, we quickly pulled the pots to the side of the boat and lifted out the crabs. Then we lowered the pots again. We kept repeating this performance until we had all the crab we could use.

Chapter 4

MISUNDERSTANDING?

$\mathcal{O}$ne evening fog surrounded our camp like a great cloud of cotton batting. My stepmother, Olive, decided to have a bath and left the window above the tub open about nine inches. There she sat in a foam of suds, happily humming to herself.

Company in the Bathtub

Suddenly a black object came streaking though the window and landed head first in the mass of suds at her feet. She gave a terrified scream which sent Dad hurrying to her rescue. He soon produced the mystery object—a dripping soapy black fog bird.

These birds, a little bigger than a robin, came by the hundreds in fog and seem to be attracted by any light. After a heavy fog, fishermen often found the decks covered with them. They invariably seemed to land in grease. The fishermen would dry them out and put them into the water again, but they always died, perhaps through exhaustion. No one ever seemed to see these birds a sea or on the shore except when the fog came.

At the end of the fishing season most fishermen looked forward to a party in the camp. At one such party a well-known fisherman, who was fat and jolly, refused to sit down at first. Finally after much persuading (he was by now the center of attention) Shorty sat down. He bent one knee only so far, however, when his pant leg began to crack, and the further he bent his knee the further the shiny black pant leg cracked, until at last it was completely off. Shorty pulled his leg out and the two foot length of dirtreinforced material stood alone like a piece of stove-pipe, while the crowd roared with laughter.

At the same party, Tuck, whom I secretly admired, kept asking me for a kiss. At that time he sported a huge bushy beard. I told him that if he shaved off his beard I would consider it—never dreaming that he would, as he was so proud of it. It was a much admired beard. To everyone's surprise, after a short absence he soon reappeared clean shaven, but he didn't collect the kiss he'd said he wanted. In fact without his beard he was apparently too shy to ask for it.

The next day was fine and I took my brother and sister to the white sand beach to build castles while I tried to get a sun tan. Tuck came over in a row boat and settled himself in the sand beside me.

He spoke of the weather and of the never ending subject of fish. Then, he said, "You know you weren't very polite to me in Queen's Cove."

"In Queen's Cove! I don't remember seeing you there." "Oh, but you did. One day I had engine trouble, I was feeling very low and you came rowing by. I said, 'Hello. Nice day, if you don't have engine trouble!' and you said 'Hmpf.'"

"I did not!" I exclaimed. "I remember now. I've never said 'Hmpf' to anyone in my life. What I said was 'Hm or "Mhm-hm"' and I began to explain the difference. Soon we were laughing and exchanging our life stories.

Chapter 5

SAN JOSE BAY

---

*O*ld-time fishermen told us that Sea Otter Cove years before had been a settlement consisting mostly of Danish people. Now where these people had lived and farmed, blackberry bushes and trees had taken over. The odd field was still clear of trees, but all overgrown with grass and high weeds.

The community hall or perhaps it was the school, we found some distance back in the woods with trees growing through its roof and windows.

On one side of the Cove we found a large patch of bamboo trees, which we discovered made ideal fishing rods. Swimming we found wasn't very good. The Cove looked like an ideal place for swimming, with its white sand and crystal blue water, but the water was much too cold.

One afternoon with nothing better to do, Tuck and three companions went to San Jose Bay to investigate an old house where a postmaster had lived years before. We had heard stories that the old man had even built his own coffin. He lived alone for many years and had died not so very long ago, possibly ten years, before Tuck and his friends had visited his house.

The furniture was all there, and a new wood stove covered with a thick layer of grease to prevent it from rusting. They also found ten bottles of home brew tucked neatly away in a cupboard. The first bottle they opened immediately emptied itself on the ceiling. The next nine bottles they were more careful with.

When they arrived back in camp they were feeling no pain. We were told later that they had nearly drowned trying to get back to camp, but they appeared no worse for their experience.

Summer came and went. In September we had the old problem to face, what to do about school. I had given up my correspondence course months before. Dad and Olive decided that I had better be sent to Vancouver for the winter to attend school there.

I spent three days on the packer coming to Vancouver. We stopped at several places along the way to pick up fish from the camps at Winter Harbor, Queen's Cove Kyquot, Tofino and so on down the line.

Chapter 6

CITY LIFE

$\mathcal{W}$e arrived in the city early one morning. With cars, buses and people hurrying along the busy streets, this certainly proved to be a life very different from our quiet lonely cove. I went by taxi to stay with my step-mothers' sister Joan and her family.

One of my cousins, Jackie, was only a year younger than I, and we quickly became friends. On my first afternoon in the city Jackie decided I should go with her to a friends home and meet some of her friends. I must admit I was surprised to find a dozen or so girls and boys all a little younger than I sitting around the living room, with absolutely nothing to talk about except the latest show and who loved who. They considered me an outsider I'm sure and said I didn't look fifteen.

I soon found out I didn't like the city life much or school life either.

The only school I had ever attended was a one-room affair with about eighteen students. We all knew our teacher intimately and in general had a lot of fun.

This huge new school I was to attend frightened me and so did the thought of having five strange teachers all at once, one for each subject!

When school opened I had a great deal of difficulty finding my way from one classroom to another. My favorite subjects, I soon discovered, were Art and Home Economics.

There were things like the huge gymnasium that I had never seen before and that were fascinating to me. I never attended any school dances. I was sure I would find them dull after the small community dances I had attended, where everyone knew everyone else and there was plenty to watch and keep you interested if you should happen to miss a dance or two.

At Christmas my spirits were brightened when I received a lovely Christmas card from Tuck, with two tiny kisses checked beside my name. It was then that I was really homesick for the West Coast.

At last winter was over, spring in the city was vastly different from spring in the wilderness, where you can see trees budding ready to burst into a new dress of green.

Tuck and I had corresponded all through the winter. He was due to arrive in the city for a few days soon and I was excited at the thought of seeing him again.

I met him at Birk's clock, where hundreds of people have met at one time or another. He told me he was going to sell his old boat and buy a new, much larger troller. When he had made the deal, I was taken aboard the new boat the SAN MARINO to view its wonders. It had a tiny galley, consisting of a rock gas range, a sink and six tiny cupboards. The sleeping quarters were downstairs—a three-quarter width bed with a locker built alongside it to hold canned goods, a tiny clothes cupboard and toilet. Tuck soon loaded the hold of his new troller with ice and was ready to set off for the fishing grounds within the next few days.

Cutting blubber from the whale

Summer holidays were here now and I was also to leave within the next day or so. I was to fly up to Hardy Bay and go from there by taxi to Coal Harbor, then by boat to Winter Harbor where my family now lived.

Tuck said goodbye to me the night before I was to take the plane, he then set off to go up the coast in the SAN MARINO. When I stepped off the plane at Hardy Bay imagine my surprise to find Tuck there to meet me! He had traveled all night in a gale of wind to beat the plane. There was only time for "Hello—Goodbye" and I was off in the taxi, speeding towards Coal Harbor.

As we reached the village outskirts we were aware of a horrible smell and as we approached closer it definitely got much worse. Coal Harbor, I soon found, was a whaling station.

Several huge whales lay plumped full of air in the water waiting their turn to go to the reduction plant. Another monstrous whale was on the beach where a dozen men gathered about and some men with hooked knives pulled huge chunks of blubber from the whales' sides.

I had my lunch in a small cafe some distance from the smell, then went aboard the small ferry boat for the ride to Winter Harbor. The ride lasted a few hours through a sunlit channel and finally into a small bay with a dozen small houses scattered along the waterfront.

This was Winter Harbor—a post office, a one-room school, three small stores and a dance hall which also served, in the winter, as a movie theater. The audience, which sat on hard wooden benches, sometimes became quite critical.

We had a house on shore this time. After only a month my family was transferred again, this time to Tofino.

Chapter 7

TOFINO—THE CAVE

$\mathcal{O}$nce again we rode the packer down the coast, bypassing our old home in Queen's Cove, and continuing on past three other settlements. Zeballos, now a nearly dead community, had once been a booming gold mining town, twenty years earlier. A few stores and hotels remained and the town was kept alive by its logging industry.

At Nootka, an Indian village mostly, there was a large cannery that had once employed many men and women but was now shut down. Remaining was a large cookhouse and several bunkhouses, all quiet and still. Off to one side were many Indian houses built up on a foundation of what appeared to be pilings. Once this had been a fierce and large colony of natives but now only a few friendly families lived here.

Ceepeecee consisted mostly of a cannery and a few houses scattered nearby. On a little jut of land a small hospital was built where injured loggers, fishermen or village folk were treated. Any serious cases were flown to Tofino or the city. Just behind the hospital a small distance, a lovely white and green hotel was built, its beer parlor the main attraction.

We reached Tofino. Our home was to be a camp again, almost a duplicate of the one we had lived in at Queen's Cove and Sea Otter Cove. We had a float to shore and we weren't long exploring this lovely place. We were amazed at the number of people living here, along with the hospital, hotel, stores and cafe.

A ten minute boat ride across the harbor brought you to Clayquot Island where the beer parlor was located. Straight across from our camp there was a tiny island with a castle built on it. We found later that the odd gentleman who had lovingly built it had drowned. Apparently three people had owned the island at one time or another and all had met fatal disaster. Many years before we were told by the town people, three Indians had been beheaded there for a crime they had committed. They were put in a cave on the island where their evil spirits were to remain forever. Their skeletons, we were assured, were still over there in the cave, if you could find it. I secretly thought that when Tuck came to Tofino that's just what we would do.

Soon were were very busy with great loads of fish to be bought, fishermen to be paid and groceries to be sold. Father and Olive were kept busy at this while I cooked and minded the children, pausing occasionally to look down the bay for the SAN MARINO.

Tofino has many beautiful white sand beaches. On hot summer days the children and I used to meet an old resident of Tofino, Mrs. Elbert and her two grandchildren. We would all go to the beach where the children and I would swim in the constant roll of breakers and loll about in the sun. Very often the fog would roll in, grayish white, misty and so very cold.

Most of the folks in Tofino, we soon found out, were related. It was unwise for a newcomer to talk about anyone, as it would invariably turn out to be his listeners mother, brother or cousin's cousin.

One bright sunny day not long after I arrived we saw Tuck's boat sailing towards our camp. He had fished all the way around from Cape Scott and down the coast to Tofino. While he was there the weather remained fine.

I told him of the cave on the island, where the Indians had been buried, so one day we set off in the rowboat to see what we could find. Before we had searched very long we found the cave. The entrance had been covered by a great deal of brush. It was about eight feet long. We found the bones and some woven grass mats that had more than likely been used to wrap the bodies in.

We brought the lower jaw bone with most of the teeth still intact, back to our camp.

When Olive had seen our discovery she wasn't much interested nor was anyone else, so the jawbone was dropped over the side and sank into the depths of the bay. A relic of the violent past though it was, I feel now that we should never have disturbed those ancient bones.

Chapter 8

THE ENGAGEMENT

---

*S*ummer was nearly over and the schools would be opening soon. My step-mother's father had been staying with us most of the summer. One day when the two of us were alone I told him that I didn't want to go back to school and would like to try to get a job. Granddad told my father of my secret plans and Father readily agreed! Soon I was to say a very sad goodbye to Tuck and of course my family. I then boarded the towns bus for the twenty mile ride to Ucluelet. As we drove along the bumpy road we passed beautiful Long Beach, stretching for miles. The sand, as fine as granulated sugar, sparkled in the morning sun. As the huge waves rolled in on the beach, several whales played and rolled about some distance out from shore.

Soon our bus ride ended at the Ucluelet Wharf. Several people and I boarded a small ferry boat, the "U-Chuck". We rode on calm waters through a lovely channel. My ride however was not enjoyable at all. I seemed to have adopted a man in his early fifties who talked constantly about his job as timekeeper at some logging camp up the coast, and the boat was so small I was unable to hide from him. I must say I spent considerable time in the lavatory.

By evening I had arrived in Port Alberni then took the bus to Nanaimo where I caught the late ferry to Vancouver.

This time I lived with my cousin Jackie, a happy go lucky soul. We shared one room on the top floor of a boarding house. Our room was small, shabby and crowded but we didn't mind, as Jackie was busy with her job and I soon to be with mine.

I started to train as a telephone operator. I thought I would never learn. In two weeks of training there was so much to be remembered.

Tuck arrived back in the city. One evening he gave me a ring which had been his grandmothers'. It was plain gold with a tiny ruby stone raising its shining head from the center. It seemed incredible that a ring could make one so happy. I went at my training with new enthusiasm and soon became an operator.

As I boarded the bus every morning a lot of dull faces greeted me, each with his own thoughts and I with mine. These people seemed content on the outside with this way of life. I wondered if they would enjoy spearing wriggling crabs or hiking over stony cliffs to find a mere few wild strawberries or being anchored in the middle of nowhere with a gale blowing. This is the kind of life I knew now that I wanted to get back to.

On days off Tuck and I spent a good deal of time together. He was employed in a coconut plant for the winter so he could help support me. I'm sure if it hadn't been for the five dollars here and the ten there I would have starved to death. My board made a big hole in my wages and the rest seemed to vanish on nylon stockings and bus fare.

We soon were to find that the city wasn't a very friendly place. One very foggy night we went to a show as we often did. Tuck took me home. Then he walked to the corner and stood waiting for the streetcar with his hands in his pockets. Suddenly a huge man grabbed Tuck from behind and threw him to the ground. Another smaller man appeared out of the fog and began to kick Tuck violently in the ribs. Tuck managed to get a couple of good kicks at the small man while he freed his hands from his pockets. When at last they were free he punched one of the men very hard on the jaw. The two thugs ran quickly into the fog.

In a few minutes Tuck stood at the boarding house door. Blood dripped from his face, the knuckles of one fist were skinned and his sides soon became a purple mass of color. The police were called. Sirens screamed in the foggy mist but the two men were never found.

Chapter 9

THE IN-LAWS TO BE

*S*oon I met Tucks parents (Tom & Helen McLeod) who had been in the city only a few months. Prior to that they had lived on a small island which they owned (Silva Bay) in the chain of Gulf Islands. There they had built their own home seven years before. They owned and raised a medley consisting of forty fruit trees, a fifty pound Tom

View from the house at Silva Bay

turkey and its mate, ten sheep, thirty chickens, two small Angora goats, a large Tom cat, two dogs and a tame deer. They had a canning house and a machine shop. Oysters grew in abundance on the large reef that the kitchen window looked out upon.

The McLeod House (incomplete) at Silva Bay

There proved to be an endless supply of fuel for the wood eating stove. High on the beach, bark and wood got tossed by the ever changing wind and storms. The twenty-five acre island itself grew monstrous firs, cedars, hemlocks and arbutus.

If the battery radio gave out, clocks were set by the ferries plying between Nanaimo and Vancouver as they came abeam of Entrance Island.

Tucks' mother led a busy life. Clothes had to be scrubbed by hand, animals fed, fruit and vegetables canned; there was the wood to cut and stack for the winter, as the men of the family were usually away hunting or fishing.

After moving to the city, she took great pride in her modern home which was spic-and-span each day long before noon. Noticing how often she spoke of the island, I asked her once if she didn't long to go back. "Heavens, no!" she replied. "Life's too short to work so hard!"

Thomas & Helen McLeod at Tuck & Willies wedding

Chapter 10

OUR MARRIAGE

I was now sixteen, soon to have my seventeenth birthday. I had been with the telephone company for several months by this time.

Father and Olive were flown to Vancouver critically ill from inhaling the fumes of cleaning fluid. Father nearly died and was kept in an oxygen tent for several weeks. He emerged from it haggard and worn, looking more like a man of eighty than forty. Olive, not being as ill, was allowed out of the hospital. Tuck visited Father faithfully. I was not able to because of the different shifts I worked. At last Father was allowed out of the hospital. He and Olive moved into a hotel to have a few weeks of rest before returning to their home up the coast.

In a few months Tuck was going to be fishing again. He told me that he wanted me to be his wife so that I could go with him. "Marrying at seventeen!" I was positive my father would say, "Out of the question!" One evening Tuck begged me to go with him to see my father to ask his permission. I said to wait till I was eighteen, as I was sure we never would have my fathers consent until then at least.

Tuck finally agreed, so I thought. The next day Father phoned me and mentioned the fact that I should put my notice in if I was going to be married in a month or so. Apparently Tuck had gone to the hotel that very night we discussed it and asked for Fathers permission, and got it!

A few weeks later at the end of April, we were married, with about thirty of our friends and relatives attending. Some friends who lived in Victoria had promised us the use of their car for a honeymoon trip on Vancouver Island. However the first morning after our marriage they phoned to say that the car would not be available until the following week. As a result we checked out of the hotel and Tuck carried me across the threshold of our boat. We scrubbed, cleaned and washed clothes the first week of marriage.

TUCK & WILMA'S BIG DAY
April 27, 1953
L to R: Doug (Dentist) McLeod), Tuck,
Wilma, Joan Hawkins

We then had a glorious weekend motoring up the Island as far as Campbell River.

Far too soon we were back aboard the boat preparing for our departure up the coast for the summer. We were going to work our way north to the tip of the Island then out to the fishing grounds.

Gear had to be put in order, food supplies bought, and many other chores to attend to.

Our first stop was to Cortez, the small island I had left three years before. We visited a few of my remaining relatives on the island, including my grandfather who was now 91 years old.

A few faces appeared here and there but the community had hardly changed, except for the new white chapel built on top of a hill.

Though there were difficulties and dangers in being a fishermans' wife and keeping house afloat I felt happy and free in my new life. This is where I belonged.

Chapter 11

FEAR ON THE WATER

$\mathcal{W}$e fished for bluebacks and spring salmon on the east coast of the Island for nearly a month, dropping our anchor at night near one of the many uninhabited islands. The greatest danger in such a position was that we might drag our anchor and be wrecked on the beach. Perhaps this was the greatest but not the only danger.

On one such evening we anchored a sizeable distance from Hernando Island. We retired to our bunk bed before dark, tired after a long day. Before long we felt our 42 foot troller list to one side ever so slightly. Tuck sat up in bed quickly and I followed suit as he whispered, "There is something on board!" From our bed we could look up the six stairs and see the back door that slid to one side to open. We always left the door open a few inches for fresh air. We soon saw a large animal pass the doorway. It slunk up the side of the boat and darkened two portholes above our bed for a few seconds as it passed.

The guns were under our bed but the bullets were upstairs in the wheelhouse. I was terrified and suggested to Tuck that he had better go up and get the bullets and shoot the animal. Tuck, being as frightened as I, realizing the risk whispered back, "If you're so damn brave, YOU shoot it."

We both lay quite still and watched the back door. Our unwelcome guest tried to stick its head in the open door but found the opening much too narrow. As we watched we soon saw that what we had on board was a large cougar, probably smelling the fish and being very hungry he had swum out from shore to see what he could find.

Finally from utter exhaustion Tuck fell asleep. I lay and watched until darkness fell and I couldn't make the cougars form out as he passed the portholes.

In the morning we found one large footprint in a small amount of left over fish blood. After that incident we kept a loaded rifle under the bed.

Chapter 12

REUNIONS

$\mathscr{W}$e worked our way further north. We then stopped to visit my mother and brother who lived in a logging camp at the foot of several towering mountains. My brother's wife was in the city having a baby.

Lawrence, my brother, drove us up the steep road to where the men logged. The narrow logging road was up the side of a mountain, below us was a deep valley with a rushing river, the Quatum, gurgling through its center.

Mother did the cooking for this small logging camp, which kept her busy baking bread, making lunches and doing all the other jobs a cook has. She had adopted a little black bear who arrived faithfully at the cookhouse door every morning for his daily handout of cold hotcakes and leftovers. It was spring and in the evenings you could hardly walk on the logging roads for the multitude of toads.

We continued on our way up the coast of Vancouver Island, bypassing Alert Bay and finally after what seemed endless hours, we arrived in Bull Harbor after dark. This harbor, as I discovered in daylight, had only two fish camps. At the head of the harbor was a government weather station, with a few brightly painted homes and buildings. Here we bought food at the store and again loaded our boats' hold with crushed ice to keep the fish as we would not be back to a harbor for two weeks.

We were going to sail around Cape Scott and I looked fondly at these last few signs of civilization. Rounding the northern end of Vancouver Island is always a rough and dangerous venture. This would be my real test, I knew.

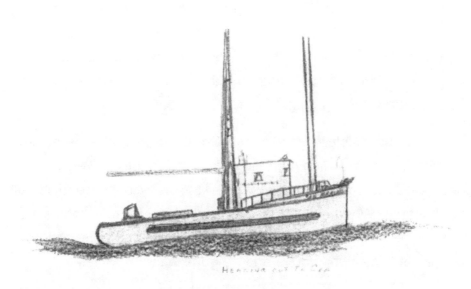

Heading out to Cap

Chapter 13

THE TEST

---

*W*hen I awoke the next morning we were well on our way to the banks. Great waves rolled and tossed the boat from side to side like a piece of driftwood. Cooking I found very difficult, I had to learn to stir the stew with one hand and hold on with the other. The top of the stove had a little fence-like apparatus built on with rods to hold the pots in place. The fence proved to be too high for the frying pan, so whenever I used this I had to hold on to it the whole time. The oven and broiler had fish cord tied around them and fastened to the wall. When I forgot to fasten the cord the oven door would fly open with a terrifying racket.

It was impossible to make a cake. Sometimes weather permitting, we got the odd pudding. On one occasion I made a lovely custard decorated with meringue on top. This I set firmly in the ice to chill till supper time. When I went to retrieve my dessert I found the ice all around the bowl colored yellow and dotted with meringue, the bowl was empty, my work of love and art gone with the waves.

Fresh water was scarce so dishes were washed only once a day and then the same water was used for scrubbing the floor. Salt water was used for peeling vegetables and sometimes also for washing the floor.

All this I gradually got used to, but not before my day of utter catastrophe. One evening at dusk when it was blowing very hard we rounded Cape Scott. I was getting the cabin ready for when we would anchor in a sheltered cove and have dinner. I had a very unappetizing watery stew on the stove with no cover on the pot. I had my back to the stove facing the sink as I was scooping up handfuls of vegetable peelings, flour and other garbage. Several dishes had been carelessly left sitting on the tiny drainboard beside the sink. Suddenly the boat gave a great lurch, The stew slopped over and scalded my leg. I jumped and dropped the bowl of garbage. In the same instant the dishes on the drainboard crashed to the floor amongst the flour, peelings, water and of course a few fish scales! I felt the whole world had crashed about me and I sat down amidst the mess and burst into a flood of tears.

At this moment Tuck poked a cheerful face in the door and said, "What's the matter, honey?" This of course bought a fresh flood of tears. However, after much consoling, I was able to bring myself to begin scraping the hardened flour from the floor and cleaning up the rest of the debris.

In miserable weather, I would spend a great deal of time sleeping and reading while Tuck sat alone and froze on deck. Occasionally, I would stick my head out the door to see how many fish we had. If we had quite a few and were getting more all the time, I would don approximately ninety pounds of clothing and descend into the swirling fog, rain or wind to gut the fish.

A very sharp knife was produced. Thumb and finger were thrust into the fish eyes to hold him still or just hold him, the knife made one sweep and the gills were thrown to the anxiously awaiting gulls or gooney birds. A quick slit up the stomach, two little muscles cut and the whole inside was pulled clean. A couple of scrapes along the back bone and fish was cleaned. He was then washed off. This performance took about two minutes for me but for experienced men it was much faster and probably much tidier. By the time I got through I certainly needed to be washed off. My face seemed to be an ideal target for specks of fish blood.

I didn't mind this job too much, but the small fish fleas on the fish, usually near the tail, I detested. They were horrible flat gray creatures that clung to the fish. Tuck, knowing my dislike for them used to tell me fantastic stories of these fleas. Once he put one on the back of my neck and I nearly jumped overboard to get it off. I must have convinced him that my revulsion from them was genuine. At any rate he never repeated that trick.

Chapter 14

STORMS

Gooney Bird

$\mathscr{T}$here were a great many birds miles out at sea. Often we couldn't see land in any direction but there would be an abundance of sea birds. One type, which we called the gooney bird, grew to a great size with a wing span of well over six feet. He had monstrous webbed feet as big as dinner platters and used them like skis. When he landed the feet were thrust forward and he skied along until he finally plunked himself down. When taking off he seemed to stomp along the top of the water. He would eat anything available, even toilet paper, being under the impression that it was food.

Occasionally little wild canaries, sparrows and wrens would land exhausted on the boats. One afternoon a little fellow landed on our boat. Tuck walked over and picked him up. We put him in a basket, he was such a beautiful little thing, a pale yellow with the odd bit of black and lovely red diamond on top of his tiny head. Of course I hoped to save him but he soon died and I must admit I cried a little when he did.

We had been fishing on the grounds only a few weeks when I encountered my first real storm at sea. Darkness fell with wind and rain slashing at us. We didn't anchor our boat but let the wind blow us back and forth all night. It was impossible to sleep. Tuck braced himself against the edge of the bunk and I clung to him. We rolled back and forth with the boat all night. About three in the morning I discovered that the mattress had handles on its side so I clung to these thinking they would hold me down, but no such luck: when the boat rolled I did likewise and the mattress followed suit.

We struggled out of our bunk early, had a cup of coffee then started for land and shelter, as the storm seemed to be getting worse.

After hours of riding through the angry water we arrived at a safe cove called Goose Island. A long string of rocks forming a reef off Goose Island were called the Goslings. There we anchored with many other boats. Some went on to Spider Island Cove where they could sell their fish and buy groceries. Goose Island was well named as great flocks of geese landed there. We hoped for roast goose but didn't have any luck.

On days like these, with nothing much to do but eat, sleep and talk, Tuck would tell me of his experiences during twelve years of fishing.

On one occasion Tuck and his friend, Norman Sear, each in his own boat, had a very harrowing experience. They had left the Goose Island banks to fish in a location called the Yankee Spot. En route they heard a weather broadcast warning of approaching storms, so they were not too surprised to find, by the time they arrived at the grounds, that all the other boats had taken the warning and returned to harbor. The weather was unsettled, unpredictable, and the sea was running high.

Against their better judgment they stopped and dropped the gear. A few hours later they were tacking back and forth, doing well as far as fish were concerned. Then within fifteen minutes the wind swung from west to southwest and increased to approximately forty miles an hour. Soon the high steep swells were curling and flying in all directions. Realizing at the same time how serious this storm was, Norman and Tuck both opened the throttle and then as fast as they could, wheeled in the gear. They made very good time running before such a wind and sea, with their own bows aimed at Mexicana Point.

There was no choice but to keep on the present course, which in an hour or more would put them on Nawitee Bar. To make matters worse, the tide was coming out over the six fathom bar at approximately five knots, bucking the southwest gale and sea. Presently they came abreast of the bar. The next three-quarters of a mile was something Tuck told me he will never forget.

The seas up till now had been high, but what they now encountered made the previous waves look like ripples. They didn't seem to move, but just stood there like mountains of water with the deepest valleys this side of nowhere.

When the little boats started to climb, the engine vibrations slowed, as if pulling a great load. Nearing the crest they would start to yaw dangerously from port to starboard, wanting to broach in the trough—which would have meant the end. But somehow Tuck and Norman managed to keep their boats dead astern. When the boats fell over the crest and drove their bows deep under the water, they were practically standing on their stems. The tons of water in the giant curling crest would break and come crashing over the sterns, submerging the entire boats, which by now were shuddering under the terrific strain and pressure, and rapidly filling up.

But something more than seamanship raised them drunkenly from the last burial to sluggishly, and ever so slowly, right themselves and pull away from the last green mountain, to stay afloat by inches only, and crawl battered into the sheltered bay.

After hearing of this harrowing escape, I wondered what Tuck thought of me for being so frightened during the few storms we had encountered.

Chapter 15

SEALS

---

*I*t was terribly exciting when we did get good catches of fish, which were few that season. On our troller there were four poles, and six lines off these poles, and then a number of lines attached to the six main lines and equipped with spoons or plugs and hooks. Two lines that came off the main poles had pigs (two three-foot canvas buoys) clipped on them, and were then let out a hundred feet or so behind the boat. When the bow poles swayed and pulled, we knew a fish was on. Gurdey handles were pushed and soon our fish came to the surface (reeled in by the motor). If he was a large spring salmon, Tuck played him carefully. Before very long he was hit on the head with the gaff, a stick with a large hook on the end: then the hook was driven through his gills and he was pulled or lifted into the boat. Tuck or I would then clean the fish. Just before dropping anchor at night Tuck would go below and securely pack all the fish in ice.

One drizzly afternoon we could see some distance behind us a huge sea lion tossing fish into the air. We couldn't catch one fish, but this large ugly creature was having great fun tossing them every which way. As we rode along, another troller pulled alongside. We were hollering back and forth, Tuck telling of the blasted sea lion that was following us and making it impossible for us to catch anything. Just then a great roar sounded behind us. There was the lion, not ten feet away. Tuck ran into the cabin, got the rifle, and came scurrying out; aimed the gun at the beast, shut his eyes, and fired!—missing him by a foot. At least we hoped the shot would scare him away to some other part of the ocean to do his fishing, but no such luck; he followed us all day, just out of rifle range.

Out here there was an abundance of seals. If a seal was shot, you collect five dollars bounty by sending the nose away. One day we shot a beautiful little fur seal that kept following close behind the boat and scaring the fish. We pulled him aboard and found he was only wounded and really quite lively. I tried giving him artificial respiration. He crawled over the side of the deck and kept pushing his nose against the scuppers, trying to get back into the water. The little fellow seemed to be suffering, so Tuck finished him off. He cut the nose off so we would be able to send it away and collect our five dollars.

After another week of tossing about we went into Namu, a large fish cannery community, to sell our fish. There I proudly showed our friend Axel the nose I was going to mail. "Holy Cow!" exclaimed Axel. "That's from a fur seal." "But aren't all seals worth five dollars?" "Not fur seals. Send that away and they'll fine you $500." So the nose was very quickly and quietly disposed of.

Gradually we fished our way down the west coast. It was lovely to be able to see land on one side of us at least, while we fished.

Chapter 16

MISSING

At Cape Cook we encountered another storm, and quickly sought shelter with a dozen or so other boats, behind a long point. On the beach lay a huge whale which had died stranded in shallow water and was quickly decaying. Two black bears stood on top of the creature eating their fill. Fortunately the wind was blowing in the right direction, so we were not getting any smell.

But before morning the wind switched, making our shelter unbearable. So all the boats rounded the point and rode up a narrow channel with huge bluffs on either side. Presently we entered a desolate but beautiful bay called Glaskish. Tuck and Bill (from another troller) and I boarded a rowboat and discovered a wide creek. We collected trout gear and pushed our way through dense bush along the bank of the creek. Soon the creek widened, gravel formed a small beach on each side, and huge log jams blocked the middle of the creek.

These spots were ideal for trout fishing. We caught two or three, which were welcome but would hardly do for supper. When we decided to head back we discovered that the tide had come in, causing the creek to back up. The large marshy field near where our boat was supposed to be, had large ditches now, well filled with water. These we had to cross. Bill and Tuck, not being nearly as brave or smart as I, stood on the bank of one of these ditches while I prepared to wade across. "Come on," I yelled; "it's not very deep!" No sooner said than I stepped in an unknown pothole and submerged up to the shoulders, while Tuck and Bill convulsed in a gale of laughter. However they had to cross, and being more careful than I, they emerged wet only to the knees. When we arrived at the large dead stump our rowboat had been tied to, we discovered it had gone.

The trollers were tied to a float a mile or so away. Fortunately we had brought the rifle along in case of cougars. We climbed up on the large stump and wrung out our socks, while Tuck blasted away on the rifle.

Presently a boy of twelve, Jimmy, who was trolling with his father that year, arrived in his small rowboat and told us how he had seen the tide coming in, and had towed our boat some distance up the creek, so we would avoid getting wet. Jimmy soon retrieved it for us. By the time we arrived back to our boats we were blue and our teeth chattered loudly.

When we were fishing I spent a great deal of the time in the cabin reading. Though Tuck often urged me to stay outside with him, I preferred the comfort of the cabin, and when the weather was miserable I would occasionally stick my head out of the door to get the score of how many fish he had caught. On one such occasion I looked out and Tuck was nowhere to be seen. I immediately went out to look for him and look I did, on top of the cabin roof, up poles and mast, and in places even a frog couldn't squeeze. I was sure he hadn't come inside, but I made a pretty thorough search just in case—toilet, clothes cupboard, under the bed, behind the engine and stairs. No Tuck.

I was absolutely terrified that Tuck had fallen overboard, which would have meant sure death as he, like many fishermen, couldn't swim a stroke, not that it would have helped much in the choppy freezing water. I was desperate and nearly made up my mind to use the radio-telephone to call "Man overboard." But against my better judgment I thought I would make one last search. I opened up the closet door and lifted up the bottoms of dresses and coats—and Tuck gleefully poked his head up and said "Boo!" I was so furious at him for playing such a trick and so happy to see him, I cried like a child. I found later, after my tears had subsided, that Tuck had fixed the phone—taken the fuse out, so that I would be unable to make anyone hear me, if I had used it. After that scare I stayed out in the cockpit with Tuck much more that I had before.

Tuck & Wilma Fishing
1953

Chapter 17

QUEEN'S COVE—THE CONCEPTION

$\mathscr{A}$fter a few more weeks fishing we arrived at Queen's Cove. There we were happy to meet our friends, Norm Sear and his wife Jaci, who had loaned us their car for our honeymoon. It was wonderful to see them again, and we had a lot of fun together. We were tied up at Queen's Cove for over a month, unable to fish as wind blew gale force and rain poured down for days. When the rain let up, we in our boat and Norm and Jaci in theirs, went up a long inlet in search of clams and trout. We found clams. Buckets full we dug and steamed, dipped in butter, a sprinkle of salt and pepper and they were devoured like peanuts.

Norman, Tuck and I went up a lovely little creek with trout gear.

Jaci stayed behind to make dinner. I had given her a pint of canned razor back clams, which had been given to me to make clam chowder. These razor backs, we were told, had a capsule in them; if this wasn't removed, the story went, all who ate the clams would be poisoned.

We proceeded up the creek in search of trout. Norm discovered a beautiful large rainbow, but he refused to bite. Discouraged, Norm handed the rod to me. No sooner had I taken it when the grandaddy struck full force. I was overexcited and called, "I've got him, I've got him!" While Norm and Tuck screeched at me to play him carefully, I lifted the pole and the fish plopped off the hook into the water and quickly swam away. I must admit Norm wasn't very happy while Tuck commented on the stupidity of women.

Later we hiked back to the rowboat and rowed out to the boat where Jaci had an appetizing pot of clam chowder bubbling merrily. We were ready to put the first spoonful into our mouths when Jaci showed us a small piece of capsule she had found in the jar.

As we had nothing else to eat, we decided to eat the clam chowder. With each mouthful we thought of being poisoned. Later when we got some of the clams, I sent several capsules to UBC, and the report came back that they were harmless. So we had gone through a great deal of mental suffering for nothing.

After this adventure we headed back to the Cove, only getting out to fish on odd days. Both boats suffered minor mishaps. One of our trolling poles broke. The next morning Norm and Jaci stepped out of their bed into eight inches of oily water. Tuck and I hurried aboard their boat where we witnessed Norm, still in his shorts and Jaci in jeans pulled over her pajamas. Jaci was using a huge dishpan to bail the water out, while Norm stood stunned in the black oily water swirling around his ankles. We soon discovered the source of the trouble. The sea-cock had been forgotten and wasn't closed which allowed the water to leak slowly in.

That finished it, we decided we'd had enough for one season. Soon we were heading for Tofino, where we stayed the winter. Norm and Jaci went on to Victoria where their home and daughter were.

Chapter 18

THE DENTIST

$\mathcal{B}$y now we happily discovered we were going to become parents. We were overjoyed to think we would have a child by August. My great worry was what we were going to do with it. Tuck was positive I could manage a baby on the boat. He had plans for building a crib alongside our bunk. He had visions of putting up a clothesline along the boom so our child could run up and down it when he got old enough, just like a leashed dog.

We seldom spoke of what we would really do when baby came, as we were so uncertain. In the meantime we settled down to pass the winter at Tofino.

Tuck found a job aboard another boat, a packer. I lived on our boat, and Tuck was with me more than he was away. The winter seemed so long and dull—it was rain, rain, rain.

One day some friends brought us a cat to care for while they went on a trip for a couple of weeks. I was excited, as I'd begged Tuck for a cat all summer. Our cat turned out to be a large, black scrawny creature with bright contemptuous eyes. Tuck wasted no time in letting me know that the cat was my responsibility.

I loved that cat—but it was impossible to put it outside because of the rain, and when the weather got rough, the cat got seasick. Finally the cat went home and I never again asked to have a pet animal on board.

Christmas came and went. On New Year's Eve we attended the community dance, where at midnight everyone kissed everyone. Measles were going around, and Tuck lectured me well before the dance, on how we would dash out of the hall at the stroke of midnight, to avoid all the kissing and measle germs which we dreaded as I had not had measles as a child.

We did as he wished. When we arrived back in the hall they were busy pulling a ticket from a hat to see who would be the winner of a bottle of whiskey. My brother Lawrence, who now lived in Tofino, drew the lucky number. The bottle was passed around the hall and everyone had a noisy swig—including Tuck, who said the alcohol would kill the germs.

One evening Tuck came dashing aboard to tell me the packer was going to Port Alberni and this was my chance to get to a dentist—something I had been wanting to do for weeks. We threw some clothes in a suitcase and set off.

By this time, in my so-called delicate condition, I got sick very easily. The voyage proved to be quite rough and Tuck was kept busy running to my rescue with the bucket. We retired to our bunk very early, so that I could suffer in privacy. I was doing just that, about dawn. The boat had picked up another passenger during the night, and there he was—in the other bunk, not five feet away. I wished I'd stayed home, maybe he did too.

The packer was to stay in Port Alberni for several days, while the captain made a trip to Vancouver. So we had lots of time to find a dentist. Unfortunately no one would take me on such short notice. By the time we had made the rounds, I was exhausted and of course convinced that I would lose all my teeth. Then Tuck suggested we go to his brother, a dentist in Vancouver. Ten hours more traveling by bus and ferry for a check up! But we did it.

Tuck's brother was very obliging, and we caught our return boat and another bus, and were back on board the packer the same day. When the skipper returned we told him we'd been to the city too. He just smiled politely and said, "Hope you had a good time!"

Chapter 19

FAMILY ON THE WAY

$\mathcal{M}$ay brought welcome sunshine to Tofino. Tuck had left the job on the packer and now began to prepare our own boat for the fishing season. He decided he would put up new poles, mast and get new lines.

I stayed behind one bright day while Tuck and three other fellows went by boat to get our trolling poles. They arrived at their destination. From the boat they spotted dozens of lovely straight poles. The prepared to go ashore, it was only then they realized they had forgotten a rowboat to get ashore with. They arrived back in town feeling very silly, each one blaming the other.

In a few weeks Tuck and I set off again in search of poles. My stomach by this time was growing large and seemed to be always getting in the way. I carried the gun in case of animals while Tuck packed the ax. After what seemed hours in the woods we emerged with four poles. We started rowing for the boat towing the poles behind us. One oar broke but Tuck very skillfully used what was left of it to struggle along to the troller.

The doctor said it would be quite all right for me to go fishing, so we left Tofino and day fished, which means bringing your fish into a harbor every night and selling them. As I was about to give birth to a child, I was relieved of cleaning fish and other duties I had done before. I was sick every day and sat on the floor, my back braced against one wall and my feet against the other. There I could see and talk to Tuck and at the same time try to knit our dear little baby its very first sweater. Despite the awkwardness and discomfort of my knitting position, this is the way I felt about the job at first—fond, sentimental, properly maternal. Unfortunately it was my very first sweater as well. I knitted from morning to night but never seemed to be getting anywhere. I kept making mistakes. When the boat rolled a little and I dropped four stitches I blamed it on the waves.

The wool got dirtier and dirtier.

The time came, however, when I was nearly through except for one row. This was worrying me terribly as I didn't know how to cast off. I tried and failed and kept trying, the rows quickly diminishing. By now in a frenzy of tears I threw my work on the floor, swearing that I would never knit again. Tuck happened to  walk in on this scene. He patiently picked up the soiled sweater and managed, Lord knows how, to fix it up very well and tied a knot so that it wouldn't run any more. He was as proud as punch which made me feel very silly and weepy-eyed. But I should have known by now a fisherman can be a handy man in almost every emergency.

Chapter 20

A NEW LIFE

*J*uly came around. I could no longer stay on the boat and Tuck was losing a lot of good fishing because I couldn't take it. I stayed a few weeks with my brother and his wife in Tofino. Then we had a telephone call that changed the pattern of our lives. Tuck was offered a good job in the city, did he want it? The money was good. It would give us a chance to make a home for our family. We accepted it very gladly indeed yet with real regret for the stormy coast we must leave.

We left Tofino and brought the troller down the coast through sunshine and fog for her last trip with us aboard. The baby only a month away, we kept our fingers crossed that the weather would be good and it was.

We finally arrived in the city, where Tuck went to work on his new job. There we lived aboard the boat for several weeks until we found

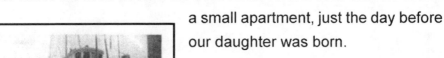

a small apartment, just the day before our daughter was born.

After some months our troller was sold to a lumber company and we settled in a comfortable home of our own.

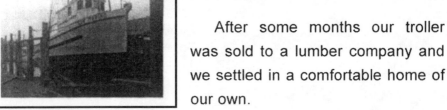

The SAN MARINO no longer fishes out in the wind and fog but chugs along on calm inside waters pulling loads of logs, while her one-time master and mate sit in comfortable chairs and sometimes day-dream of bygone days.

The life we lead now is the only kind for people with a family, and we enjoy it—and yet we often look back fondly to the life we had on the West Coast.

SECTION II

NEW YEARS IN THE WILDERNESS

The Cabin

Chapter 1

THE DECISION

---

*K*en our twenty-one year old friend and neighbor, my fourteen year old son and myself make an unusual trio as we traipse the backroads together. Besides sharing a common birth month and the zodiac sign of "Pisces" we all love the spirit of adventure, exploring and of doing something "different", such as bottle digging, picking wild asparagus or seeing where a road or trail will lead. Over the past few years we've talked to naked hippies (male and female), been lost miles in on a backroad, the truck stuck hub deep in clay. We've seen the beauty of wild flowers, mountains and streams, uncluttered by people and civilization. We've traveled considerable miles, been cold, hot, tired, lost, bedraggled and begrimed. We've seen the beauty of the Alpine meadows, the silent wonder of the forest at night. We know how natures elements can change ones personality, but most of all we have shared much laughter!

Our trip of trips to date, has to be the winter of 1978/79.

The one thing we hadn't done was camp out in the winter—it's something I'd wanted to do. What was it like to sleep out in the snow? No far off plans are made for our trips, they never are—as we go on the spur of the moment, when the opportunity of escape is available.

I have a very understanding husband, who thinks I am slightly nuts. He doesn't enjoy sleeping on the ground or eating soot covered meals from over a camp fire. He does however love the backroads and trail biking, plus the beauty of nature so seems to understand my need to leave our comfortable home at times and take off for the bush.

Mark, our youngest son, Ken and I had "in fun" discussed what it would be like to spend Christmas at the cabin—the cabin being abandoned and window free, was thirty miles in behind Lillooet, a little log shanty we'd stayed in for a couple of nights last summer. The idea had been kindled, wouldn't it be fun to spend a couple of nights there before the New Year? I asked Ken, could he go? "No" he had other plans, he and three friends were going to Loon Lake to spend New Years in his parent's cabin. So that was that for the time being.

The next day December 28th, the plans were called off by the friends, now we're able to go. This would give us Friday night and Saturday night at the cabin, we would be able to be home Sunday afternoon in time for me to get my hair done and be presentable for the New Years Eve Party that Tuck had already prepaid $50 for tickets.

I called to Mark "get out of bed, we're going to the cabin!" I asked Tuck if he'd mind if we went—"not at all, but take lots of food you may need it, and check in with the R.C.M.P before going in there." was his reply.

So the rush was on to get ready. The temperature here was—10 up where we were headed Lord knows how cold, plus a five to six hour drive to get there. We weren't even sure if we could get into the cabin, there may be too much snow.

Chapter 2

PREPARATION

I dragged out the pack sacks and started to fill them, while Ken and Mark took off in the truck to buy Mark a new pair of boots and some warm wool socks. We also needed to pack slide films, socks, sweaters, gloves, warm sleeping bags, old quilts, two wool blankets, small feather pillow, old sofa cushion, tea kettle, fry pan, plates, cups, cutlery, matches, toilet paper, flashlight, extra batteries, coal-oil lantern, plastic pail, ax and shovel. Our food consisted of an assortment of goods on hand, (bread, frozen t-bone steaks, frozen hamburger, eggs, bacon, garlic ring, one package chicken noodle soup, one can soup and fish, freeze dried chicken, margarine, one can milk, cocoa and sugar mix, can of corn, candy and nuts. Mark threw in his little gas stove, extra white gas, large piece of heavy black plastic, his new green tarp he got as a Christmas present plus two chucks of foam rubber. This was all loaded into the back of Kens Toyota truck and we were off.

The sky was blue, the air cold and the anticipation of a new adventure stirred abundant conversation. "Will we be warm enough? Did we bring the chains? How deep will the snow be?" were questions asked. Yes we did, plus Ken had new studded snow tires.

What if the cabin has burned down? What if hunters are staying there? We'll sleep in the tent—God Forbid!

One hundred miles later we stopped for gas at Hope, also to buy some cough candy for Mark. He had a sore throat. "Don't worry Mom I am okay." he said. I bought some chocolate, that left me one dollar and twenty-five cents. Kenny had thirty dollars and an Express card, anyway we didn't need any money where we were going!

We're off again. Snow now appeared on the sides of the road, huge waterfalls were frozen solid, the bottom of the falls sometimes frozen in mid-air as if caught by a giant cold wave before the water could reach the ground. It was noticeably colder, the Fraser River had patches of ice, large icicles hung from the steep gray rock bluffs. The road was ice and snow free and we sped along.

Soon we could see the aerial ferry swinging high above the frozen Fraser River, its drifts across to the other side to North

Waiting for the ferry

Bend. "That looks like fun, keep going!" stated Mark . . . too late we're already turned around heading for the ferry. Ken asked the girl attendant if the dirt road on the other side went through to the Lytton ferry . . . it did. We drove into the red cage and a steel door snapped shut, a jerk and a dip and we were swinging high above the ice crusted river. By the time I got my camera out of its case and focused we were on the other side. Ken drove off, up an icy road then across railway tracks. There was a choice of two roads to take, no road signs so we took the one to the right.

The sun was shining brightly. The ice that covered the road looked about five to six inches deep, it was like driving on an ice rink. The ice gleamed green, blue and silver in the sun, the snow laid in thick white patches of down on the many evergreens. The road twisted and turned. We stopped the truck to get out to take some pictures, but soon hurried back into the warmth of the cab as our breath made white clouds around our faces.

Chapter 3

ICE

The road began to get worse, switchback turns and hills. We turned down a steep grade and approached a wooden bridge, we stopped to admire the slowly moving green stream, banks of ice closing it in, the frost was hanging in white delicate fingers from tree branches. As we started off again the wheels of the truck slipped off the main planking on the bridge onto the spaced beams, but we managed to get back on the planks again. Before us loomed a hill, Ken tried to zoom up, but no dice, we slid back down, zoom again this time we got to the top. We encountered different roads, and had to back track after making several wrong turns.

The next steep hill we only got part way up and could go no further. I got out. Mark and Ken backed slowly down. I broke off tree limbs and threw them on the ice. I had to stay on the side

of the roadside in the snow, as once you stepped into the main roadway it was so slippery it was almost impossible to stand . . . what a place to sleigh ride. Ken, Mark and the truck disappeared from view and didn't return. I slipped down the hilltop to find Ken in the process of trying to put on the chains. Darkness was fast approaching and the cold completely penetrating. We could see headlights of cars shinning across the river on the main highway and wished we were one of them.

A freight train rumbled and grunted by below us. We thought the ferry stopped running at seven p.m., Ken was trying to hurry so we could get back to North Bend and get on the main highway again. But no good, the chains wouldn't fit. (Ken had bought new tires since he last used them). It was decided we would make the ferry without them. By the time we got back to the wooden bridge Ken had a change of heart and said "I have to get these chains on!" I proceeded to build a fire with some cardboard from the beer case and some wet sticks. While I was busy, Ken and Mark jumped in the truck and disappeared again. The fire finally started to splutter and the boys didn't return. I walked up the hill in the dark and saw the truck.

I was completely out of breath from the short climb, as I reached the truck. Ken said, "I've got to find a more level spot to put these chains on!" With that he promptly hopped in the truck and roared off again, making it to a spot a little further up the hill. Meanwhile I again puffed up to where they were. Mark was sitting in the truck, his feet so cold they were numb. Ken was busy doing something with a shovel. It was pitch black, but the sky was alive with a million twinkling stars. I again proceeded to try and get another fire started. Intent on my quest, the next thing I know I hear the truck rumbling off down the hill around the corner and out of sight. I muttered to myself "for Gods sake" and stomped down the hill after them. Ken by now was busy looking for the shovel . . . which of course was still back up the hill.

Mark was utterly miserable with cold feet. This time I got the fire going in the middle of the road, Ken was removing tires and having an exhausting time trying to get the chains on—I admired his perseverance and patience. Mark got off his new fur lined useless rubber boots, got on warmed socks and hiking boots that were too small. It was a steady job to keep feeding the fire, climbing up the snow bank pulling out old roots and snapping off limbs.

Ken and Mark

Chapter 4

TENTING

---

*T*his procedure went on for about two hours. Finally a white bearded humpbacked figure, leaning over a tire and chain requested food.

Everything was frozen solid. The only liquid we had was liquor, even the beer lids had lifted off the cans. I took the frozen garlic ring and tossed it (paper and all) into the fire, slowly the paper ignited and burned away, gradually the outer skin was a deep black. We munched on the sooty outer skin, the inner meat still frozen. One chunk remained, no one else wanted it, so when it looked heated through I took a huge bite and ended up with a mouthful of meat plus an abundant amount of sand and gravel from the stump roots! While I gagged and spat, Ken was triumphant and succeeded in getting the chains on.

We left the small fire glistening and crackling on the bed of ice as we drove off. We were again happy and anticipated no more problems, we figured we'd drive the next sixty or so miles through to Lillooet, over the cliff hugging Texas Creek road.

We got about four miles . . . then approached a big hill. We nearly got to the top when we saw some buildings—a house, barn and outbuildings nestled under the trees all in darkness. The road seemed to lead directly into the dark little settlement, so we sheared off to the left. The road was now not only icy but also snowy. Slowly we proceeded vertically sixty feet then could go no further. The truck slowly slid off the road. I jumped out—"What are we going to do now?" Ken jumped out of the truck "Are you crying yet Wilma?" (fully expecting me to be).

We all decided to push . . . and the truck slid miraculously back into place. I had visions of it taking off like a sleigh to the bottom.

Slowly we backed down . . . two feet . . . one foot . . . stop . . . two feet . . . one foot finally we reached the bottom. "Now what!" We couldn't drive ahead as it was now too late to get the aerial ferry back. All we could do was tent out!

We drove for about a mile, and found a fifty by fifty foot clearing at an intersection of two roads. Ken and I outvoted Mark who wanted to get closer to North Bend and camp near houses. Ken placed the truck so the headlights shone onto the clearing, so we could see to put up the tent. Mark was still cold and was now mad. We tried to spread the big piece of crisp black plastic, but it was so brittle it didn't want to co-operate, and the new green tarp, Marks Christmas present (from his Aunt and Uncle), exploded into an assortment of pieces from the cold. Ken put the aluminum tent pole in place. "Hold it" he said, "while I get some string". I pushed the pole into the snow, it snapped and broke. "Oh Hell" I shouted. "What's the matter?" Ken yelled from the truck. "I broke the bloody tent pole!"

Chapter 5

FREEZING TO DEATH

The tent went up after a fashion, it drooped and dipped and was shorter in the front than in the back, but it was partially erected.

I hauled the bedding into its cold black depths and made up three beds, across the frigid lumpy floor. The flashlight had disappeared, so Mark lit the coal-oil lantern, which smoked as the wick was turned too high. Ken gathered wood, soon the flickering fire turned into a roar of flames, caused from the monstrous fir limbs piled one atop the other. Fortunately the big limbs snapped off the trees easily, and it kept us busy doing just that, to feed the hungry flames.

We melted snow in the little aluminum pot, and when we found our cups, we put in instant coffee, the warm snow water in which fir needles, ash and cinders floated, added liberal amounts of brandy and warmed our spirits and our bellies. There was nowhere to sit, so we stood as close to the fire as possible. Great clouds of smoke billowed past the tent, scattering fly ash and cinders over the snow. In a few minutes our drinks were cold, so it was off to gather more wood. The heat from the fire felt good, our fronts were warm but our backsides froze, so it was a slow rotating sort of stance that we performed.

The brandy gone we decided to crawl into our deep freeze beds, not a pleasant task. Mark in the middle was warmest, as he and I cuddled close together, but where my body touched the ground it felt like solid ice. Sleep came swiftly . . . as did awakeness two hours later . . . about two a.m. I awoke to a feel of cold that felt as if the marrow in my bones had turned to ice. I pulled on my boots, teeth chattering, and making low moaning noises (like in childbirth) I crawled from the tent into the black glacial night. My inner fear of darkness and wild animals was pushed to the back of my brain as I staggered down the road looking for wood. Soon I had a fire going. "Are you all right Wilma?" Kens muffled voice asked. "Yes, just freezing to death!

Ken crawled out, together we gathered more limbs and wood, and presently Mark appeared. We melted more snow and made chicken noodle soup, which we all agreed was delicious, even if it did have a slight wood brandy flavor. Even though the soup had tasted good, and the fire was burning well we were all tired and miserable. We thought if we made a communal bed we may be warmer, plus put extra bedding under us instead of over us . . . we'd give it a try. Not very eagerly we left the fire to crawl into the cold bedding, ice crystals glistened on the walls and ceiling of the tent, sparkling like rhinestones in the flickering fire light and the light from the smoldering coal-oil lamp. Again as my side touched the floor the penetrating cold was instant.

The snow under us had melted in patches from our body heat and lumpy hollows were felt. Marks arm under my neck felt warm, hip and thigh cold and my feet warm as they were tucked beneath Marks legs. Ken had a small piece of foam under him so didn't feel the cold under his body as much, but he didn't have anyone to wrap around for body heat, as a result he was completely miserable and didn't sleep. I dozed as did Mark for about an hour, and so the early morning hours passed.

Chapter 6

TIME STANDS STILL

---

*O*ur next anxiety was to see if the truck would start. Mark lit his little gas stove, Ken heated the oil pan, and she crankily turned over. The packing of the tent, bedding and plastic was done as quickly as possible, and we found the flashlight under the tent.

Now we were secure in the cozy cab of the little Toyota, headed for North Bend and the ferry. Once we were swung high above the river and on the other side, we fueled up and found the temperature had been—30 . . . . not a wonder we were cold!

"Are you sure you feel like driving all the way to the cabin?" we asked Ken. "I didn't come all this way not to" was his reply. "What if we get there and someone else is in it?" (no one would be that nuts) "What then? Can you drive all the way back to Vancouver?" "Sure" was the answer. "Because NO WAY am I sleeping in a tent again!" I said.

We admired the Sumac trees along the way, tufts of red resembling lilac flowers graced the tips of the bare branches, looking vivid against the white backdrop. Pearly everlasting flowers thrust their heads above the winter blanket, everywhere everything was frozen, ice and snow glistening in reddish sun. The Fraser River was like solid ice.

We turned off the main road, and began our trip on a dirt road surface into the Yalakom Road. We had twenty-six miles on a road that leads to Bralorne, so we would only be approximately six miles onto the Yalakom road. The road was now snow free but icy in places. We stopped for a few moments to admire the Bridge River rapids, the ancestral fishing grounds of the Lillooet Indians, now not much of a rapids, just monstrous chunks of ice crunched together.

A road sign read 'Warning avalanche area for the next 8 km.' We didn't have to worry about a snow avalanche too much, but huge frozen boulders loomed menacingly over the roadway. Little ski runs in the slide areas showed where rocks had run down the snowy slopes. When we reached the huge erosion bowl on the left side of the road, we were too cold to get out and inspect its magnificent depths.

Ken swung the truck to the right, the Yalakom River road, almost immediately we were driving in snow. A vehicle or two had been on the road before us, so we followed along in the snow ruts, approximately nine to ten inches deep. The cold seemed more intense and increased the beauty of the woods. "What time is it now Ken?" It was still 12:10, and we all laughed. Now we had no proper time, the watch had stopped, so we'd have to guess.

Snow had raced down the steep hillsides gathering more large mounds that looked like doughnuts along the roadside. It was a very admirable sight to behold.

Chapter 7

THE CABIN

 $\mathscr{F}$ our miles in on the road we came to the Yalakom river . . . in summer a roaring white crested blue rush of water . . . now a quiet green stream, ice islands on each side, trees bowing to its loveliness dressed in white frost and snow. We crossed the slippery log bridge and began the incline, two more miles to go. We had to make this hill . . . up, up, then we could go no further, and we began to slide back. "How close are we to the edge?" Ken inquired. "Too bloody close!" Mark and I yelled. Slowly we backed down the slippery white incline, the green river far below. Ken stated "If you two climb in the back for extra weight we may make it". Mark and I climbed into the back of the truck, laying atop frost shrouded bedding, boxes and pack sacks, praying through blue lips, we made the top of the hill. We jumped into the cab, enthusiasm again filled our conversation. "We'll get the stove going in the cabin and have steak. We'll be warm!"

Down another hill, over another wooden bridge that sat atop a frozen stream, around a rock bluff and we could see the cabin through the trees. I saw someone or something run behind the cabin . . . "Someone's there" I said. "Where, where?" came a double chorus. "It went behind the cabin" I said. Ken drove the truck through the snow towards the cabin, one set of human footprints led the way. Ken leaped from the cab and rushed to the door, peered in then shut the door. "Don't cry Wilma" said Ken. "Why? What do you mean" I replied in panic. "There's someone—here all their stuff is inside". "Don't tell me that, you're lying" I said as I pushed past him to open the door. My eyes quickly took in the fact that Ken was joking and that we would be the only occupants!

The cabin, approximately 12×12, was dim inside. Plastic covered its three glassless windows. Someone, bless their hearts, had made a new stove since last summer. A forty-five gallon drum had been cut in half and welded, a damper put in its front and a good size hole in its top to push wood in. There was a tin lid to fit over the hole, a solid stove pipe reached four feet up through the ceiling and a piece of tin surrounded the pipe on the roof. A knife cut in the burnt wood showed where the roof had been temporarily on fire. Under the little window next to the stove the logs were charred from the stoves heat. The table, four feet from the stove was made of several planks, one end nailed to another window, two pole legs supporting the other end. A solid layer of mouse stools covered its top. One old rickety kitchen chair sat against the other plastic covered window, a piece of cardboard covered a hole in the floor. Another chair, made from a solid piece of wood by a power saw sat by the table. A partial roll of tar paper lay on the floor underneath a twelve foot platform, built three feet off the floor, wide enough to sleep two, long enough to sleep four. A piece of shag rug 3×4 lay on the floor.

A block of cedar to use for kindling sat atop another small platform, a few cans of assorted frozen cans of food sat along the wall on the ledge of the logs. A two litre container of frozen milk above the doorway dated Dec.2nd (someone had been here a week earlier). A small shelf leaned out from behind the stove, a small broom and clothesline completed the decor.

Chapter 8

OUR STUMP

$\mathscr{W}$e started a fire in the drum stove atop the many ashes, then we all began to search for wood. We hauled limbs and sticks, then found a nine foot rotten stump which we knocked over and carried chunk by chunk back for fuel. The old stump burned the hottest, and we found we needed to only use a small piece at a time, it was so full of pitch that the stove literally roared. The stove pipe turned red hot as did the front and side of the drum. The black smoke poured from the chimney, causing the snow to melt. The melted snow dripped down the outside walls, causing long icicles to form. The mouse dirt was swept from the table and a cloth was laid . . . its blue and orange flowers looking completely out of character. The cast iron frying pan held three t-bone steaks that soon began to melt and sizzle, the browning meat smelled good to our nostrils. The onion, potatoes and green pepper were too frozen and hard to cut so were thrown in with the meat as is, and with the lid on they soon began to cook.

We walked a hundred feet to the river, it was a magnificent sight in the dimming daylight. Islands of ice near the narrow flowing stream were of different shapes and patterns, the thick ice near the shore had a pattern of intricate designs of snowflakes painted over its top.

The big ax made echoing sounds in the still cold as Ken chopped through the several inches of ice to reach the water. Mark held the back of my coat as I held Kens . . . just in case. We drank as miniature ice chips were already forming inside and out of the container. We gathered more wood as darkness swiftly approached.

Two candles were lit, stuck in old wing bottles, the coal-oil lantern was hung on a nail above the table, the fire was warm, near the stove. Our steaks cooked. Ken and I poured a gin, mixed with lemonade concentrate and mountain water, in which natural cubes bobbed.

Supper was superb, the gin was superb, the company delightful, the cabin looked cozy (although really wasn't) the gin had distorted my mind. "Too bad we have to leave tomorrow, this is really fun". Three small drinks of gin in my tired body I was bombed! I made up the beds, then hurried back to the stove. The frozen ground beef and our one can of milk was thawing on the shelf behind the stove. My ski pants had developed several large holes caused from the heat of the stove. The canned milk fell on the floor, and as I reached to get it, my sleeve and the front of my nylon jacket brushed the hot stove. Now my coat matched my pants—three great gaping holes let the down feathers float freely. The boys were in fits of laughter as I swore and tried to find my needle and thread to pull the hard cooked nylon material together.

Every few minutes we had to open the cabin door (which let out any heat at all we had) to scoop up snow in the pots to throw on the hot wall. The melted snow formed a puddle around the stove in which bark chips and rotten sawdust from our stump floated, dolted now with down feathers.

Chapter 9

THE PILLOW

$\mathscr{B}$edtime was growing near, we guessed it to be about eight o'clock.

Mark was trying to warm the round sofa cushion for his bed. Presently Ken said "Something is burning". I could see a brown scorch mark on the pillow Mark held, so told him, "Be careful. Better still I'll sit on it to get it warm".

A short time later we could all smell an indescribably rotten odor. It was traced to the pillow on which I was sitting—it was on fire inside! We were all laughing now. I tore open a little of the material—the little pellets inside were smoldering and the stink was unbearable. I took it outside and put it in the snow.

The boys were yelling "What a rotten smell, bury it! Bury it"! So I kicked a few inches of snow over the odorous round. Twenty minutes later the smell again enveloped us, and by now I felt sick. "How can three small gin make me sick"? I demanded to know. "Well the coal-oil lamp was dripping in your drink once" Mark stated!

Out I went knees down to the bitter cold snow to rid myself of four dollars worth of scrumptious t-bone steak. Meanwhile the boys were yelling "While you're out there get rid of that bloody pillow"! I gingerly picked up the white, stinking, belching round and carried it forty feet from the cabin and buried it deep in the snow. Once we were in bed the fire died quickly—we were cold but at least there was no snow under us. We had to be up early, had to get home. I had to wash my hair, press my dress, remove the soot and get ready for the New Years dance. Yes we would be home early—sleep overcame all thoughts very soon.

Surprisingly enough we all awoke at the same time, maybe because we were all cold and the smell that engulfed us was unbearable. It was pitch black in the cabin and the ungodly stench of the pillow permeated our nostrils. Complaining we all got up and got the fire going. Now I had to go to the bathroom. Coal-oil must be a laxative mixed with gin, at least it sure felt like it as I rushed to find the toilet tissue. Half undressing in the cold black air was bone wrenching. While I was going about this whole nasty business the boys were yelling "GET RID OF THE PILLOW!" In the night air I could see the white plume of smoke billowing from the nasty thing blowing towards the cabin. When I went to investigate I called to the boys, "It looks just like Mt. Vesuvius!" Black cinders had erupted out of the snow mound, spewing ashes several feet. Again I buried it.

The sky was black but the stars shone with a brilliance I'd never seen before. We calculated (by guess) it was about 3 a.m.

Chapter 10

UNANSWERED PRAYERS

---

*W*e had cooked the ground beef the night before, placed the lid on it and put it on the floor, to be reheated for breakfast, but in the dark Mark had tripped over the pan scattering the contents amongst the mouse dirt and wood chips. All that now remained were a few frozen crumbs in the greasy pan, and on this we placed the few pieces of bacon we had. The eggs were useless, frozen and split, so we had toast, bacon and hot chocolate, once we thawed out again. The warmth of the food and fire made us all realize that we were still tired, but not tired enough to cross the room and crawl into those cold, cold beds. At last we decided we would be able to get away as soon as daylight broke, so we would be home early in the day.

Ken brought the battery in from the truck and sat it on the block chair by the stove—this was turned regularly so it could warm. Next he drained the oil into our four liter plastic pail, dumped it carefully into pots and cans, which he then warmed on the stove, and redumped back into the plastic pail. Our life-blood, which this nearly was, couldn't have been handled more carefully. Everything now should work just great . . . but a gnawing doubt filled all of our minds . . . would the truck start in this extreme cold?????

The cold gray dawn approached. I packed the bedding into the crisp plastic bags. The quilts felt damp-cold, all was made ready for our departure. Ken put the warmed battery back into the truck, then the oil. "Please God let it start" I prayed. A low moan came from the trucks throat, then it rested—moan—Another short prayer, but it was no good.

Visions of my patient husband throwing fifty-eight dollar tickets for the dance out the window, now not so patient, filled my mind. My stomach began a series of knot-cramp dances. Friends not speaking to me, more cramps, more prayers . . . .

Ken put his head under the hood and gave it another try, but the engine couldn't turn over. "Boil water" Ken said. I kept the fire roaring as Mark and I collected snow. It took twenty minutes or so before the snow was melted and the water hot. Finally Ken came in nearly frozen with a rubber hose in his hands, he began to suck goblets of ice out of it, the fuel line was frozen. "The water's hot Ken" I said. "That's good. You know what they say in an emergency—boil water" he exasperated! It was either laugh or cry, so I laughed. He did use the water, several batches of it, but to no avail . . . now the battery was nearly dead . . . up until now I had hoped so very hard for the truck to start, not even for myself so much, but for my husband and friends I felt I was letting down. Now I knew it was hopeless. I thought well . . . here we are—there is no hope of getting home for New Years Eve . . . because we can't, now what? A million thoughts crashing through my head all at once!

It was then that one of the nicest boys I would ever know in my life walked into the cabin. Ken—with his beard hanging in white crystals, his feet red with cold, as he removed his socks and rubbed his numb toes, he asked, "Can you think of anything else I can do"?

Chapter 11

KEN TO THE RESCUE

---

*W*alk out for help, we decided was all that could be done, and Ken was the one to do it. Mark wanted to go too, but would have held Ken up mainly because his feet bothered him so much. It was about six miles to hike in bitter cold and snow to a road where the odd car does travel and another twenty miles to Lillooet. Ken had a sandwich of cheese and a cup of hot cocoa and warmed his socks and boots. In his packsack we put his sleeping bag (not a very warm one), a bundle of matches, paper, stumpwood (it was light and dry) sunflower seeds and candy. I gave him a note to call Tuck and tell him where his good clothes were hanging if he went to the dance. Ken said, "I'll tell him you and Mark are nice and warm at the cabin". "Oh sure" I said. "Well no sense worrying him" he replied. "Okay" I agreed.

"Now if I don't get back tonight don't panic" Ken said. "We'll stay right here and collect firewood, but you'd better get back tonight" I stated with a note of panic. I grabbed a cardboard box, and Mark and I walked him to the road. "Good Luck Kenny, see you later" I said holding back the lump in my throat. I felt like a part of me had walked away. I was so concerned about Ken that whenever my thoughts went to him, my stomach responded in a series of sharp knotting cramps. One part of my head said . . . what if he twists his ankle, tires out completely, doesn't get a ride after the six mile hike and has to walk twenty miles?????

I found a good cache of wood, bark chunks and old limbs under a snow mound, left by a bulldozer, I'd imagined. Mark now began disturbing symptoms, severe stomach cramps (nerves I was sure) and the runs. He was cold and had no color. "Where do you think Ken is, Mom"?

"Oh probably in a car or having coffee some place". "What if he sleeps by the road and freezes"? "He won't, don't worry—Ken is just fine".

Mark and I ate some canned salmon, which we first thawed in some warm water—that along with some thawed burnt toast and cocoa filled our stomachs. My concern for Mark and Ken were the only thoughts upper most in my mind, the fifty-eight dollar tickets seemed a hundred years ago. Mark was cold and tired. I made up a bed using all the bedding in a single sleeping bundle, into which he crawled and fell asleep. I sat alone in the quiet grayness, dropping chunks of bark into the fire. The only noise was the occasional roar or hiss from the burning wood and the deep breathing from Mark. I looked at my hands, full of cuts, scratches and black with dirt. I thawed my hand cream and managed to massage some of the dirt off. Then I heard an engine outside . . . I opened the door in great anticipation . . . no one, four times I swore I heard Ken coming, opening the door to find nothing but stillness and cold, now my mind questioned, are you going nuts or is this called wishful thinking?

Chapter 12

WHAT WAS I THINKING?

*M*y mind and body felt better if I was doing something, so I went in search of more wood. The sound of coyotes calling far off spurred me on. There was no way I wanted to have to go out after wood in the darkness (because basically I am the worlds biggest coward). Mark awoke after an hour or so numb with cold. He tried to help me get wood, but his cramps were too miserable . . . I wanted to boil some water for him, so we took the axe and Mark chopped a hole in the ice. I boiled the water hoping he would drink some, but he refused to put anything into his stomach as he kept feeling as if he were going to be sick.

The limbs and branches were piled to the ceiling in one section of the cabin, several box loads of bark and an old washtub of wood filled the corner. Darkness crept over the cabin like a cold black blanket.

The fire crackled but produced almost no heat. Mark seemed worse, and he fought to keep from retching. I tried to be cheerful. "Isn't this something Mark, you and I here together for New Years Eve?" I kissed his face Happy New Year. He wasn't impressed.

I finally made up a bed on the floor near the stove. I'd hung all the bedding from the rafters to try and warm them, but they were anything but warm. I sat close beside Mark as he huddled in the bedding. I dropped pieces of bark into the fire and encouraged him to sleep. "Do you think Ken will be back tonight Mom"? "No, I don't think so". "But we'll freeze if we sleep here again". "No we won't I'll make a nice warm bed and we'll be just fine". Mark dozed off for awhile. My back was near his head, and with his arm around my waist I sat with the cold penetrating my bones.

My thoughts at that point were . . . What the hell am I doing here? I am a nutty 42 year old menopausal grandmother, sitting in the middle of nowhere, freezing, all alone except for my sick fourteen year old and the howling coyotes . . . I could be home right now getting ready to go to a fancy dance. Well this is what you wanted—winter comfort—better make the best of it.

What if Mark gets worse? What if he has appendicitis? How could I get him out of here . . . the heavy black plastic, I could pull

Wilma and Ken
"Are we having fun yet?"

him out on that—all 190 lbs of him, six miles over ice and snow . . . there, now I felt better. I had decided I could do it if I had to. Where was Ken?

Mark awoke, we talked for awhile then decided to make the bed up on the platform and try to get warm. I took great pains in making the bed. I placed the pack sacks against the wall (for protection from the draft that came in), all the plastic and the old rug off the floor went down first, heavy quilt, double old sleeping bag, double wool blanket partly under us and the rest left to fold over the top. Part of it I nailed to the wall above our heads for more draft protection. Over us were two part down bags, a small wool blanket and the remaining sections of the other bag and blanket. We warmed our feet and socks and crawled in fully clothed in jacket and hats. We cuddled as close as possible together and were just tolerably warm if we didn't move and kept the bags over our hatted heads.

Chapter 13

SAVED!

The stove quickly became cold, the night was black and silent. Then I heard a noise. I felt Marks body stiffen, then another noise . . . "Did you hear that"? Mark whispered. "It's likely a mouse" I whispered back. He relaxed. Forms of grotesque creatures floated before my closing eyes. Then we heard an animal walk past the cabin at our heads. Marks breathing halted, so I knew he'd heard it too. We listened . . . it moved again. I hollered and Mark let out a roar, it was probably a coyote or coon after our discarded frozen eggs outside. No way I was getting up from our partly warm bed to find out, and I thought, "The door is locked with the hook on the inside" so we drifted back to sleep.

I awoke with a sudden jerk . . . the roaring of a truck engine was right outside the door. "Mark! Mark! Ken is here!" he lifted his head and mumbled, "Good Ken is here" and fell back to sleep. I jumped out of bed, threw some damp wood and cardboard into the stove, lit the candle and tried to get the fire to go, but it went out. I opened the door to a blaze of light from the trucks headlights. There stood Ken and two men. "About time you got back here, Ken" I called. The men peered at me. Ken grinned and shook his head, "Wait till I tell you about today". He came to the cabin door. I kissed him Happy New Year.

Never have I been so delighted to see anyone. The stove refused to go. The men followed Ken in the door. Ken said "Wilma I'd like you to meet Len and Ron." Both men looked in their early forties. Len wore a fur hat with ear flaps, Ron was gray haired and friendly.

"God look at all the wood" they commented. "Have you had anything to eat" they inquired? With Rons help the fire finally started. Mark got up and was suddenly fine. I repacked the bedding. The men and Ken were going out to the truck then into the cabin to warm their hands, one trip in and Ken asked, "Where is the bottle of Scotch?"

We all (except Mark) had a drink of the thick liquid from plastic glasses, toasting to a Happy New Year. "Okay, let's go" someone called. I rode in the cold truck with Ken, Mark piled into the warm '66 Fargo four wheel drive that was to tow us out.

The little Toyota's windshield was thick with ice, so Ken had his head out the window to steer, long icicles forming on his beard. He was trying to concentrate as I badgered him with a hundred questions. "How long did it take to walk out? Did you get a ride? What time is it? Who are these men? Where did you find them? Did you talk to Tuck? What did he say, was he mad?"

When Ken wasn't concentrating too deeply his story unfolded.

He'd had an enjoyable hike out, hitched and got a ride when he hit the main road (miles from where

Ice-bearded Ken

he'd started). A young couple stopped and picked him up, thinking he was an old white bearded prospector with packsack, and were quite amazed to find he was an ice bearded young man. They drove him to Lillooett . . . There at a garage (Len) volunteered to drive him back and tow us out. When they came to the hill at Yalakom road, he couldn't make it so they went to the nearest ranch where Ron lived. At one point there were several men going to come, but it ended up with just the two coming. Finally the Toyota's engine started and the tan rope was released.

Chapter 14

HAPPY NEW YEAR

$\mathcal{R}$on invited us to his home for coffee. The power was off so the cozy ranch kitchen was lit by a coal-oil lamp, the oil stove put out a warmth I'd forgotten existed.

Feeling very foolish and looking very grimy we were treated to coffee and coke. Mark suddenly was fine as he gulped his coke declaring it the best he'd ever had. Ron would only accept a minimal charge for the tow out, and we were very thankful for their help. Len was supposed to be home for dinner by 6 o'clock but it was now after midnight, a bright New Year ahead. Len left for a much delayed dinner, and after thankyous we piled into the Toyota's warm cab to drive the 20 miles into Lillooet. Now we needed gas for the truck and no gas stations were open. We had no hope of getting home without it, so another room was the only answer. Mark phoned his Dad. I refused to enter the motel office New Years morning looking like a witch.

Tuck was busy at 1 a.m. installing a new bathroom basin after consuming a few rum. The next day he was to discover it was several inches out and had to be redone!

Hot showers, clean sheets and warmth drifted us off into a world of deep sleep.

We arrived back in North Vancouver in the afternoon of January 1. Kens Mom had a delightful Turkey dinner awaiting us all. How appreciative one becomes of everyday things we all take so for granted.

It was a New Years I never forgot. Friends say why do such trips?

I say, "Why not, if nothing else it makes one aware of what you are capable of doing, and it makes our citified bodies and minds more aware of nature. One learns from experience. Mark says he'd never do 'that' again and really isn't too enthusiastic about my trips now—however a year and two months later we had begun to explore the Natural Hot Springs we found . . . . That is another story!

WILMA

Hair of white,
Eyes of green,
Always twinkling oh so bright
The most wonderful smile ever seen.

A Mothers' hug, a squeeze so tight
To her breast she holds you near,
Through the day or late at night,
You know you're safe with nothing to fear.

The bond of love runs very deep,
Although apart we are never alone,
For the bond is with us even when we're sound asleep,
from the moment of birth till we are fully grown.

I miss our days of laughter and fun,
Our talks and walks for miles,
Enjoying our trips in snow and sun,
But most of all I miss your smiles.

When I have been down and out,
I know you've come to me,
You give me inspiration it makes me want to shout,
Thank you God for giving me the ability to see.

Although the persons body is gone,
Their spirit is very much alive,
Generations after us will live on and on,
So save a spot in Heaven Mom, until Home I do arrive.

—Susie—

SECTION III

THE KOOTENAYS

Trout Lake—South Kootenays
1993

Chapter 1

THE DUMP

---

*W*e have been here for ten days now—Norm working at the pulp mill and when his shift is over, we explore.

The days are long in the camper by myself. I've read and painted, washed my hair—enough of this it's time to go outside. I've walked the shelf above the river, picked up rocks, panned for gold, watched the train speed down the tracks. Examined wild mushrooms that I've never seen before, found some 100 year old bottles but broken in half. In the tall dry grass under Larch and Pine have spied where deer lay down to rest.

The Rockies loom up beside us as the sun sinks in the sky. It casts a pink light against the shaggy Pinnacles just as a full and bright moon rises above to mingle its yellow glow intertwined with the pink of the sun—what a glorious sight.

Norm and I walk up a road, laden in the thick dry dust, a sign "Refuse Site", oh well, it's quiet and beautiful. We walk much further than planned, beyond the dump and more. Norm discovers an old railway right of way and follows it along, picking up spikes from old timers that have lain on the mossy ground a hundred years or more. The rail road is easy to follow, mounded several feet above the natural lay of the land. Pine, fir and larch dot the open meadows and one can see for thousands of feet beneath the branches. The larch will soon lose their fir like needles, but for now are brilliant yellow. Mixed with oranges, reds and browns the woods are a marvel of color.

Darkness is soon upon us, the moon in all its yellow glory bouncing light from one crazy hilltop to another. We speed our footsteps, a long walk awaits us, morning comes early and so does work. Hands entwined we speed our pace.

Shots fill the quiet night air. People are shooting at the dump. God knows at what or where. Norm hollers out in the dark stillness, "Watch your shots, we're here!" Bang, bang was the only reply. "Are you deaf you dumb bastards? Hold your fire!!" He hollers again and again and finally the shots close. As we approach nearer the site, we see headlights glaring, what is their target we do not know. Except for the lights it is dark and silent. Norm calls out, "Hello, hello!" We just get by then the shots begin, my partner shudders as if hit within. "Dumb buggers" he mutters. We hear their truck begin to roar, as our footsteps move faster in the dusty dark. We duck into the trees and let them past. Crouching beyond a patch of juniper and pine, the truck comes roaring, spewing dust in the moon light glow. As it reached the spot where our footsteps glide into the bush, the vehicle slows and stops, I whisper "Oh no" but after a moment it speeds on its way and so do we, free from bullets and come what may.

Chapter 2

EXPLORING

---

*W*hen Norm was at work one day I walked along the rivers edge and spotted across the river old houses nestled in the bush and trees. When he gets home I thought we'll explore. We walked the road but the only way in was along the railroad right of way. Walking the tracks made me nervous as hell, as the trains speed by here full tilt. "Don't worry" Norm says, "we'd just jump over there!" "Oh sure", I reply as I eye boulders, steep hills and trees. Soon we are where we can climb down off the track, through head high weeds to the old shacks beside the flowing river. Darkness is fast approaching, the buildings are old, but hippies lived here in the 60's, papers galore. I picked up some books and a spoon. Walls falling down, old tables and chairs. Four buildings, what a story they could tell. We must leave, darkness is falling fast.

We drive up the mountain past rivers and fields, climb through a fence and walk on mushroom laden moss to see an old railroad bridge. It's still standing, cross beams hanging, the deck rotted out, the same line Norm discovered a few nights before. A splash in the river diverts our attention, there in the crystal blue stream dozens of red Kokanee are swaying in the gentle current, awaiting to lay their eggs and die completing their two year cycle. Along the road climbing and twisting, we look far below to Premier Lake, reflections of yellow trees dancing on its blue-green surface. Here in this quiet spot we spend the night. We open the skylight and the moon shines in, stars twinkle above our heads and as we snuggle in the warmth of each others bodies, it's a wonderful feeling and we soon doze off to the stillness of the night.

Canal Flats, Fairmont Hotsprings, huge condos, lawns, fancy buildings, rules and regulations, park here, not there, pay here, go there, we're not impressed, but hundreds are.

Whiteswan Lake, beautiful and still, puddle ducks bobbing for food. Alice Lake still and pure, we climb to the top of the world park. Gravel road . . . higher and higher up the magic mountains until we are enclosed in their rocky arms. Through what they call the "Ram Burn of 83 Valleys" and mountains burnt in a fire that must have been hot enough to melt hell. Amid the charred black and beached white standing trees, weeds and seedlings struggle to become a forest again.

Far below a river winds, the gleaming yellow of the larch making this disaster almost beautiful again. Roads here, roads there, roads everywhere. We talk to a hunter and he tells us to watch for a hot spring along the way. It takes us awhile to find the right road (for none would ever put up a sign).

Chapter 3

KOOTENAY BEAUTY

---

*T*he sun is warm, hard to believe this is October, we've seen no grouse which we find strange. Then there it is!!! A warm creek, algae and all, spewing down the rocky mountain side.

We climb a billy-goat trail with the warm sun on our backs, then what a magnificent sight. Perched on the mountain side two pools of blue, clean, sparkling warm water, gravel bottom surrounded by boulders. All to ourselves. We bathe and we swim with delight in the natural beauty of this spot. We hate to leave, but it must be. Norm starts his 12 hour night shift starting at seven, bending and fitting tubing. The mill has been on shut down, quiet and still but tonight steam and noise shatter the night as they prepare to reopen.

Campbell Lake tiny and small, not far from Wasa, a rest spot really, that's all. The yellow, greens and reds reflecting in the mirror water, broken only by big trout jumping, which very soon we had in the black cast iron pan fried to a golden pink, devoured by us in hardly a wink.

As I sit here and wait for my man, I write. I think of the places we've seen here in the Kootenays. The ghost town of Sardon, crunched in a narrow valley between towering mountains, a creek running through the center of town where they had built. All flooded and gone now, except for a few buildings. High up the hillsides as you crane your neck to see are workings and tailings. The town was big, railroads, hotels, fire hydrants, all swallowed up by time.

New Denver was my favorite place. Old, quaint, clean and quiet, houses all different large and small. Nestled beside the lake, maple trees blazing the colors of Fall. Here we picked apples from the ground and munched as we drove, juice running down our arms.

Fort Steele, mostly redone, was open now for the season. We and one other couple strolled through town. North West Mounted Police barracks all made of logs, hotels, houses, dentists and barber shops all several blocks long and wide. Houses furnished, some barren and bleak, some with lace curtains, gardens and all. The cobblers shoes looked so small a five year old would find them too wee today. The same as the dentists chair, being so narrow an adult of this day would not be able to get his behind in it. Several old apple trees still bloom there producing apples so small and sour. Hat makers, saddle makers, bakery . . . it was all there. Four thousand people once roamed the boardwalks, all gone now. It looks all romantic and great, but I'm glad I didn't live then. The houses so small, wash tub hanging on the wall, wood to be cut, bread to be made, winters cold and bleak.

No radio, television, phone or mall.

Chapter 4

OH HAPPY DAY

---

*O*ctober 6, the worst day here for me. The first day it has been cloudy and dull and the cold feel of Fall I felt in my bones.

Norm arrived back here at 7:40 am and offered to take us some miles up the road so I could fish and he could sleep. I knew he was tired, an all night shift, so I said no. So here I sit wearing two sweaters and a coat—watching as the cars go in and out. Norm sleeps peacefully for awhile, wakes, grins, snuggles back down and is off to nowhere land again.

I've read and I've read, my eyes grow weary, cooked up a mulligan of green pepper, onion, hamburger, tomatoes and mushroom soup. Made sauce of apples getting wrinkly skin and done crossword puzzles by the dozens. It's 4 p.m. now so will let him sleep another half hour more, then off he will be all night again. I hope this doesn't last too much longer.

The mountains look distant today, bathed in low cloud, the trees have lost their sparkle of a look forlorn in the grayness of the day. My feet are cold. Now if I didn't smoke I could warm it up in here.

But no . . . complain of the cold and have another smoke, what an idiot I am. Norm looks so peaceful in sleep, comforter tucked up under his chin, I wish he didn't have to work tonight.

Trucks, cars of all kinds, men big and small coming and going, a constant move of shifts, men just coming and going. The steam from the mill making its noise day and night. The odd sprinkling of rain I now hear on the roof. Chipmunks and squirrels still gathering food as they race up and down logs on a mission so true. Grasses gone to seed, cones hanging in clusters on fir tree branches. Purple Asters still bloom but mostly everything is waiting for winter to come.

I was sad as Norm went off to work, the lights seemed so dim to read (now it couldn't be glasses so old, or eyes so weak!) What a surprise should await at 9:45 as I peered out and look, Norm arrived—"Sweetie I'm home, the mill has shut down, no power." Delighted I was to have and love my man.

No work until 7 p.m. the next day, so off we go at 6:30 a.m. drove in the darkness to Cranbrook. Headlights facing all the way, car after car on their way to work. We drove all around town, spotted places we wanted to see. Into the Assay office for maps and breakfast (I didn't have to cook, but would have done better.)

Off to Maggies, a sweet little gal who sold paint, canvasses and oil, there I purchased two canvasses to paint, she charged only $10 but it should have been $16. Hope to see you again, off to the Royal Bank—"Oh where are you from?" "Sechelt", we said. "Well how is my daughter?" the clerk replied. I looked at her—are you weird or what?!! "My daughter lives there and works at the Blue Heron or baby sits". "A small world" we sighed.

Chapter 5

HOMEWARD BOUND

We shopped for groceries, new running shoes in the mall, off to the liquor store rum for me and shooting sherry for Norm.

We stopped by the river with banks all in white clay, had three drinks then drove to the mill. Now Norm is dozing and supper will be ready soon. Corn on the cob bought in Kimberly, big red fat tomatoes, roast beef, gravy and fresh bread. For dessert we splurged, two big pastries filled with strawberries, cream and curd.

7 p.m. and we've eaten it all! Our bellies are full. Norm is off in the pale evening light. I watch him as he fades from sight. The mill is quiet and still, maybe he'll be back. I'll keep my fingers crossed. It's slightly overcast, the night still, guess I'll put my pen down and crawl into the cozy down comforter.

"No work—all finished" Norm declares and I'm glad, to bed and in the early morning off we'll go.

Drive we did. Fairmont Hot Springs, passed the Voodoo Cliffs into Radium Hot Springs for a look. Watching scenery change as we go. Mule deer grazing in fields by the road. Train tracks winding on its seemless endless course. Into Golden for fuel, trucks and cars all in hurry now. Into Revelstoke, clean and pretty, then through

Rogers' Pass (can't believe kids on bikes in the tunnels). The mountains are beautiful, snowsheds, colors of Fall everywhere.

Traffic everywhere finally onto a quiet road to catch the Gallino ferry across the Arrow Lakes. Trying to find the ghost town of Beaton was hard, then discovered it was under the lake. Off of Trout Lake, a big town in its day, now only a few little places like the old store with glass gas pumps. The lake is long, lovely and full of big trout. We camp here for the night beside a small trailer that a bear or man has broken into. We try and repair the damage for Trapper Bill best we can.

Quiet and starlight we sleep like logs in stillness. At daybreak we're off to Ferguson, a ghost town of long ago. We drive a narrow, twisting dirt road, scary for me as I peer down hundreds of feet to a river and pray we don't meet an on coming vehicle. We pass by a clearing in the woods, not realizing this was Ferguson, on we go, the road getting narrower and steeper. Now we have to turn around. God, I can't look! We get back to the clearing and spy a couple of old places in the trees.

We're off in the frosty dewy weeds up to our armpits, climb into the woods where we find an old dam. Treasures! An old shovel head, a pot nested in the pine needles up against a tree and an old milk can full of dynamite sticks. Norm checks "okay" he says, so we pull them out by the dozens. How man years have these been here? Then I spy a dump, never dug, lots of beautiful glass, but nothing whole! I'd love to stay here longer but we must leave . . . .

Chapter 6

THREE YEARS

---

*W*e're off to Gerrard. We drive the east side of Trout Lake, dirt road all to ourselves. Colorful, scenic and spectacular. Gerrard is all gone too, except for a couple of abandoned places, old apple trees and shards of glass in a dump where I'd love to dig for a week.

Norm backs the truck and camper under a 100 year old apple tree laden with fruit, climbs up on the camper and picks a big box of blemish free delicious apples. The camper is beginning to fill up, bottles, glass cans, apples, shovels etc. etc.

We decide we'll go to Trail to visit Ken and Elaine (my niece), so we drive to Leards River Poplar City (ghost town) where the Kokanee spawning grounds are. Into an old marble mine then Kaslo, New Denver.

Now there is not much room in the camper so we get a motel in Salmo, where we have a bath in the hardest water in B.C.

We arrived at Ken and Elaines before noon the next day. Lynne (Elaines sister) was there for Thanksgiving, so we had a nice visit. They wanted us to stay (she was having 22 for dinner the next day) but we said no, we had a nice lunch with wine then were on our way by 4 p.m.

Over to Rossland, then through the Cascades on an old dirt road (for the scenery) switch back up and down two mountain ranges, across creeks and rocks then darkness. A flat tire! Luckily on the only level piece of ground. In three hours driving we saw 2 grouse, five deer and a lynx. We finally switch backed down the mountain into Grand Forks. We then drove to Greenwood where we climbed over a spare tire, apples, bottles etc. etc. to get into bed! Left early for home, finally back to the traffic and hassle.

It was good to get home. Arrived at Susie's for a turkey dinner which was great. It was a lovely trip and "I" plan to go back next Fall.

October 27, 1993

Our third anniversary today, no regrets—only love and happiness.

Of course we're getting ready for another trip. Now . . . first we were going to go fishing and Grouse hunting then . . . read an article about pine mushrooms at Terrace.

Now, we'll probably not see an animal, Grouse or mushroom but anticipation is high. Spareribs, stews, chili, spaghetti, and steak are all prepared. Our only problem is, wouldn't it be wonderful to have a camper clean from clutter!!! We are going to try this time . . . . but . . . . when it gets down to the nitty gritty, where do the pack sacks go (for mushrooms)? Where does the power saw go, oil, gas, rain-gear, fishing gear, the rope, the chains (it's nearly November), so to hell with it!

Chapter 7

MUSHROOM PICKING

*P*ile it all in! It will be like always, full up, not fancy free. We need a trailer, we want a quad, we want a lock up trailer, we want a winterized camper, we want to retire, we want to be 30 again. The only thing we don't want for is to be happy, we are lucky, we already have that and it's the only thing that doesn't cost us any money!

It's 9:10 p.m. of course I am already packed, precooked, etc. etc. and Norm is still bungy cording stuff on the back of the camper, God bless him, he is far more organized than me. I might be ready faster than him, but when someone falls through the ice Norm will have the equipment to save him. All I could do is throw him a marinated chicken leg!!

We're off. The weather has changed, not for the best, so what I'm looking forward to it all. We hope to stop at the farm in Prince George, fish hunt and mushroom pick.

Prince George, Houston, Burns Lake, Kitwanga, Terrace nearly up to Stewart, rain, rain and more rain. Tried to find the road to Cranberry Junction where all the pine mushrooms were supposed to be. Finally after a day and a half we found the area, now deserted of all the pickers. Their mess of garbage littering the otherwise lush green moss woods. The mushrooms were over.

We caught big Rainbow trout in Dragon Lake. A family of four otters spotted us and came swimming over to us, cavorting and snorting their strange language, begging for fish remains. I was completely taken by how tame and fascinating they are.

The road, a sea of mud, bridges washed out. Finally we near Nass camp, Aynish and the lava beds. Mile upon mile of boulders, no trees or vegetation, only boulders covered in white algae. A moonscape of mist, rock and desolation. We hunted for moose in behind Houston. Waking in the morning to a blanket of snow. Driving in the morning darkness we followed footprints of two bear who had staggered down the road ahead of us. The day after the moose season closed we saw a big bull but that is not unusual.

The camper now is in its usual state of dirt and disarray after two weeks of mud, rain and snow but it grows on you after awhile.

We have our "Happy" hour or hours, bonfire at night. Admire the stars when we can see them. We go across the Fraser River at Big Bar onto a narrow steep road that climbs for five miles straight up (15% grade) the mountain. 4x4 in full low, the camper nearly hitting the wall of rock and clay beside me. The switch backs so severe if our unit were any longer we'd have to backup. God forbid! I was terrified!! Never could another vehicle get past if we met. My heart finally began to pump blood again when we reached the first plateau.

The scenery spectacular. Mountain Sheep graze along the river benches, the little ferry a speck below us. A flock of Chukkers fly up beside us. Beautiful, but I'll never take this road again!!

Chapter 8

PRINCE GEORGE

---

*W*e spend two days at the farm in Prince George. It's been two and a half years since we were here. Someone broke into the shed and stole our weed-eater. A woodpecker drilled dozens of holes in the outside wall. Several big ones, so Norm sheeted them over with plywood. We plan to come back here and spend more time, build a fence and do some fixing up in the near future.

Finally it's time to go home again. The house looks inviting and clean. It's always good to get home, but in no time at all we're talking about another adventure. There's Christmas to get ready for. Hopefully work for Norm soon.

Then plans for the Queen Charlottes next summer, mushroom picking near Nass camp and only try and get that elusive moose.

CPSIA information can be obtained at www.ICGtesting.com
Printed in the USA
LVOW090430180412

278021LV00001B/1/P